CLOVIS ACADEMY LEGACY

BOOK TWO

THE FORBIDDEN REGION

Ross Harringway

FORBIDDEN REGION

CLOVIS ACADEMY LEGACY:

FORBIDDEN REGION

OMEGA PRESS

An imprint of Omega Communications Group, Inc.

For information contact:

Omega Press
5823 N. Mesa, #839
El Paso, Texas 79912

FIRST EDITION

Printed in the United States of America

FORBIDDEN REGION

PROLOGUE

2532 The Year of Sikorsky

It was a horrible way to die.

To be slashed, torn, ripped and mangled was one thing, but to be eaten alive by a pack of creatures was another. And then, there was the primal fear that all humans have by instinct, the fear of being eaten alive. But this death was not one that occurred by chance or misfortune, it was a staged execution for a man that had dared to disobey his masters. The man that was condemned to die was named Carlton Rand. He was twenty-two years of age and a slave of the Rosenburg family. Carlton Rand had been born into poverty and was abandoned at an orphanage on Sikorsky's Planet when he was only four years old. Rand remembered little of his mother and nothing of his father. He spent two years at the orphanage until he was sold to the man known as Alfred Rosenburg the Second. Rand was flown in a space craft from Sikorsky's Planet to a planet that had been named New Edinburgh.

Rand recalled the flight in which he, along with dozens of other orphans sold into bondage, were taken to their new lives to serve the Rosenburg's. The long flight past solar systems, asteroids and other space craft was an exciting experience for the young lad. He always remembered the beauty of the planet called Osiris which was a multi-colored gas giant in the same solar system as New Edinburgh. Rand remembered standing by the observation windows as his transport ship passed the colossal planet and wondered if any human life could be sustained on her surface.

Many of the children from the orphanage did not understand the transaction that had occurred as they were too young to comprehend what was happening. Rand was six years old when he had been sold. He had heard that slavery was illegal in the laws of the United Nations of the Earth Empire and secretly hoped that one day he would be freed by the law enforcement officers of the Space Command.. Rand and the other children were to learn quickly that the Rosenburg family did not have to obey the laws on human slavery. In fact, the Rosenburg's obeyed very few laws. The Rosenburg family had money, power, influence and cared little for others. Due to their vast influence, the laws of the local, state, planetary government and the United Nations were optional for them.

Over the years, Rand learned to accept his life as a slave to avoid the beatings and other harsher forms of punishment. Rand was first assigned as a house cleaner at the massive Rosenburg Mansion which was located on the Rosenburg's Ranch Territory. Rand did such an efficient job, that he had been transferred from house work to learn to be a trainer of animals and other slaves. Rand was given more liberties as a trainer was a prestigious position in the Rosenburg hierarchy. Rand had been sixteen at the time of his promotion and was allowed to have the pleasures of a slave girl in his bed.

As Rand aged, he had been able to observe the Rosenburg Ranch grow. He experienced the population expanding and witnessed the construction of amazing buildings with state of the art architecture. Rand knew the Ranch covered a large land mass and had a labyrinth of underground tunnels for the family to hide evidence of their illegal activities when the infamous law enforcement officers would come to town. When Rand had arrived on New Edinburgh, the Rosenburg Ranch Territory had only settled about five percent of the entire property allotted to them by the Glorious Leader. By the time Rand was to executed, the Rosenburg's had tamed about thirty percent of the land. Rand had seen the Rosenburg family expand their landing strip for space craft from a single hanger and concrete strip to fifty hangars and dozens of strips and massive paved areas. Rand observed the Rosenburg family increase as Alfred Rosenburg, II, took more wives and produced more children. Rand had been allowed to attend the weddings of some of the children who created grandchildren for Alfred Rosenburg, II. Rand was honored to teach the children of his master the importance of safety around animals. He had been a part of the slaves that organized the celebrations for Alfred, III, when he returned home after graduating from law school. Likewise, Rand participated in the planning of the festivities to honor other

FORBIDDEN REGION

Rosenburg children when they completed medical school or other higher collegiate successes.

Rand had been taken to the southern portion of the Rosenburg Ranch to assist in the construction of the Rosenburg Corporation missile and weapons manufacturing buildings. The land mass for those massive factories covered about forty square miles and had many buildings towering over ninety floors high. Rand observed the construction of giant nuclear missiles, laser canons, laser rifles, laser pistols, thermite bombs and grenades, concussion weapons which would turn the insides of a human to jelly, armor piercing rockets for small one man space ships and the Raumschiff Transports. Rand was a part of the security teams that guarded the construction of rockets with nuclear capability that would be a part of the armament for the giant military Battle Cruisers of the Space Command.

Rand was also one of the slaves that assisted in building the holding cells for the human and alien servants. Rand felt safe due to the fact that the Rosenburg family had constructed massive walls of steel and concrete to keep the giant dinosaurs in the jungles from breaking into the Ranch Territory. In the early years, many human settlers became meals for the indigenous creatures. After the Rosenburg Ranch walls were finished, the deaths by the New Edinburgh monsters decreased. The walls did not stop the occasional sand spider, which would wait under the purple sands of New Edinburgh to leap out onto their prey. The venom of the sand spider was deadly to humans. The sand spiders were known to grow as long as three feet, moving five times as fast as a man with their eight long legs and showed no mercy. The walls also could not stop the giant earth worms that would tunnel underground and occasionally surface, wrap around a human or animal and crush them like a boa constrictor might and drag the carcass under the coarse sand of New Edinburgh. Then there were the six to twelve inch long blood sucking insects that would venture into the Rosenburg Ranch seeking a person to feed off of. Lastly, there were the twelve foot long giant flying red and green colored four winged predators called Cawlers. They were named Cawlers as that was the sound they would make when they would swoop down on their prey. The Cawlers had a wing span of fifteen feet, six black eyes with square shaped yellow pupil's, four long legs with long claws that they would use to snatch the hunted on the ground and fly them to the red-orange sky and peck the victim to death with their razor sharp beaks.

Rand was thankful, as were the other slaves, when the Rosenburg family installed force field screens on the large protective walls that would repel the Cawlers. The flying giants were intelligent and realized that the laser based force shield could not be penetrated and they discontinued their hunting on the Rosenburg Ranch areas. However, the Ranch had many exports and imports which required the force shields to be dropped during business hours for space craft to land and depart. On rare occasions, a Cawler would attack during those time periods and some unfortunate person or animal would become lunch.

Rand had seen many years of the Rosenburg Ranch history. He always tried to do his best to prove himself to his Masters. So, when the family finally rewarded him the pleasure of women, Rand was pleased. One of the slave girls given to Rand had been one of the women that the Rosenburg's referred to as their "breeding stock." Rand had seen such women come and go over the years. The Rosenburg family leader, Alfred Rosenburg the Second, was a lecherous old man. He had several wives, a few dozen lovers and even more slave women that he used for his sexual urges. In addition, the patriarch of the Rosenburg family desired to work on his number one goal in life which was to expand the number of his children. His vast medical staff would artificially impregnate many young women that had been captured to spread the Rosenburg seed. The unfortunate women would have their eggs harvested, with Rosenburg's sperm, and then the women would go through the in vitro fertilization procedure, sometimes the women would do so to protect their families from reprisals, others would do so voluntarily and others by force. The women would be watched by security guards every hour as they carried the children of Rosenburg to term and give birth. Most of the births were triplets, quadruplets or even more. He was well over a hundred offspring and close to hitting the two hundred mark.

After the "breeding stock" woman gave birth, they were then either used again and again for breeding purposes, or they were given to a life of luxury as a Rosenburg wife, or they were committed to a life as a slave on the Ranch. Many of the breeding stock women learned quickly not to break the rules. It was an unspoken rule that if they wished a life devoid of beatings they would have to submit to every demand on them to please the Rosenburg clan.

Due to his loyalty and hard work, Carlton Rand had become a favorite of the family. When he turned twenty-one years old, Alfred Rosenburg the Second gave Rand a gift. He brought Rand to a large hall in the Rosenburg mansion and informed Rand that he deserved a wife. In the hall were seven beautiful women, sitting in chairs, their heads down as they refused to make eye contact with any other person. Rosenburg informed Rand that these women had been part of the latest "breeding stock" and had already given birth too many children for him. Rand was grateful that he would be given a wife. That was the second best honor the Rosenburg's could bestow upon one of their slaves, the highest honor was being given freedom which Rand had seen happen only twice in his many years living on the Rosenburg Ranch.

Rand inspected the women and one of them caught his eye. She was so beautiful, yet she had sadness in her eyes. Rand knew she was the one for him. He pointed the woman out and told Rosenburg that he chose her.

FORBIDDEN REGION

Her name was Jenna Taylor McAdams. She was also twenty-one years old. She had given birth to three children for Rosenburg. When she saw the handsome man point her out, she stood up. McAdams had not given up hope on returning to her home on Earth, where she had been kidnaped from, to be a part in this mad mass breeding. McAdams' mind wandered back, to how the nightmare had all started.

Jenna Taylor McAdams had turned twenty years old and was celebrating with her friends in Cabo San Lucas, Baja California Sur, on Earth. It was the greatest time in McAdams' young life. She was turning twenty and celebrated that milestone by drinking, dancing and enjoying the view of the beaches and the vast earth ocean. While she and her friends walked from bar to bar, she had many men that were competing for her attention. McAdams had never drawn so much attention from men before. Although she was an attractive woman with a boisterous way about her, she had only one boyfriend back in her hometown of Chicago. But it had not been a serious relationship as it ended after only a few months. McAdams went out with her friends on the fourth night of her seven day vacation when something horrible happened.

Jenna Taylor McAdams had been kidnaped.

On the night of her abduction, McAdams had been drinking heavily at the popular bars located near the beaches of the popular tourist city. After a few hours of tequila shots and margarita's, McAdams felt dizzy and disoriented. At some point,

McAdams became separated from her friends. She searched around the packed bar and concluded that her friends must have left her to visit another hot spot. She decided to get back to her hotel room on her own. McAdams believed she had drank too much and just needed to sleep off the liquor. She staggered out into the streets and slowly walked in the direction of the resort hotel she and her friends had rented for the week of celebration. She never made it to her desired destination.

McAdams remembered being offered a ride in a space craft by a handsome man in a nice business suit. She made the mistake of accepting. The man guided her into a grey metallic colored space ship that was hovering above. She felt the man assist her up the walk ramp. There was a woman there as well that helped McAdams. She remembered being taken to a plush couch and safety restraints were applied by another man and then she fell asleep.

Jenna Taylor McAdams regained consciousness over a year later. She found herself on a hospital bed in a strange room. She squinted her eyes due to the brightness of the lights in her eyes and could see several other people around her. As her eyes grew accustomed to the lights McAdams looked closely at the others in the room. There were doctors, nurses and she saw a familiar face, the man from Cabo San Lucas, he was there as well. He had a set of green military clothes on and had a laser rifles slung over his shoulder. He was standing next to a life size gold statue of the Glorious Leader, Vladimir Sikorsky. The doctors were discussing "the patient" and "the baby." McAdams tried to speak, but her voice would not make any sound.

The room was large, with light blue tile on the walls. The ceilings had solar light panels which illuminated the entire room. McAdams made her best guess that the dimensions of the room had to be over three thousand square feet. The floors were tiled in an off-white color. She saw a flight of stairs that led to a second level where there were computer control panels, and several other people, all wearing blue suits, typing in date on a three dimensional holographic keyboard. She observed other people talking, exchanging notes.

She felt nauseous and dehydrated.

McAdams arched upward, but she had restraints tied to her arms and legs which prohibited her movements. She cried out but no sound would come from her mouth. She noticed that there was a needle in her left arm, a strange green liquid in the tube attached to the needle. McAdams wondered why she was being medicated. Her mind was racing with questions. Did she become involved in some accident? Where was she? If this were a hospital, where were her parents and siblings? Where were her friends?

The man in the military clothes leaned over her and smiled. "She is awake,"

A man in a blue uniform leaned over McAdams and shined a light into her eyes. "Do not worry Miss," the man in blue reassured her as he inspected her eyes and then checked her pulse. "I am Doctor Cush Rosenburg. You are quite safe."

McAdams looked up at the Doctor and found him to be very handsome, tall with short blonde hair and blue eyes. He looked young for a Doctor. Cush reached out for a plastic cup, pulled out a few small pieces of ice and placed the ice in McAdams dry mouth.

"Just allow the ice to melt and swallow the water," Rosenburg said softly. "You had a very long trip and were in cryogenic-sleep for some time."

McAdams was now even more confused than before. Cryo-sleep? Long trip? She never recalled her vacation plans including anything other than a trip to Cabo San Lucas. Cryo-sleep was technology used for long voyages into deep outer space. Any human or animal that entered what was known as a cryo-sleep tube would be rendered in a state of suspended animation and would wake up only if the cryo-sleep tube was opened by another person, or the computer on the cryo-sleep tube was programmed to open at a certain date and time. She had never been into outer space and never had any plans to leave Earth. She had been studying for her degree in History of Earth religions and had been an exemplary student, achieving perfect marks in all of her classes. But none of her studies involved space travel.

McAdams felt that something was very wrong. She should not be in this place.

FORBIDDEN REGION

McAdams sucked on her ice pieces and the cold water in her throat felt divine. McAdams was at least at ease due to her throat feeling much better.

"Where?" McAdams asked softly.

Cush had been listening to the woman closely. "Where are you? You are in my private medical facility on my parents' property. We are taking very good care of you and your children."

"Children?" McAdams frowned. She had never given birth in her life. In fact, she had never been pregnant.

"Yes," Doctor Rosenburg nodded. "You are pregnant with triplets."

McAdams began moaning and had a look of bewilderment in her eyes. She recalled that she had sex while on Cabo San Lucas with a waiter at the hotel she had been staying at. She had been cautious in her sexual encounters; she took birth control capsules regularly, even though the pills were illegal under United Nations law. The supplier of the pills always swore that they were guaranteed to work so there was no possible way she could be pregnant. She looked down at her stomach and noticed that she was large in that area. She began breathing heavily as if she were about to panic. She watched a nurse inject her with something.

"You are going to give birth to three children for my father," Cush told McAdams. "You should be honored that my father selected you for this gift. All of my siblings are wealthy and successful and my family is very powerful. Your children will grow up to be Generals, doctors, lawyers, political leaders and masters of industry. Your children will be descendants of the Glorious Leader, Vladimir Sikorsky."

"How?" McAdams wanted to know. She did not remember sex with a Rosenburg man while on vacation and she certainly did not recall any man attempting to pick her up at the bars or beaches she went to that claimed to be a member of the Royal Family. McAdams was bewildered as she wondered why could remember.

As if reading her mind, Cush smiled, "Yes, yes. I know you have millions of questions. You see, Dell Ragnarsson, the man you met on Earth, was sent by my father to find women suitable to procreate with and make more offspring. Mr. Ragnarsson brought you and a dozen other women from Earth for the procedures."

"What?" McAdams felt the drugs from the injection she received working. Her breathing began to slow as she felt calmer. "Procedure?"

Doctor Rosenburg walked around his patient. "The in vitro-fertilization. My father's sperm and your eggs which we implanted six in you. Three attached. We kept you unconscious to ensure that the pregnancy would take. The other eleven women had similar successes. Only one woman suffered a miscarriage. My father is very pleased."

"Why?" McAdams felt warm tears running down her cheek.

"Why you?" Cush asked. "Because we wanted young, attractive and intelligent women to breed with for my father. You and the other eleven were investigated thoroughly. You were one of our top candidates. My father had frozen hundreds of sperm samples when he was much younger. My father had vision. He had wisdom beyond all of us on this planet. My father's bloodline must be spread to many."

McAdams began to believe the young doctor was saying these words to convince himself, and not her, of his actions.

"Planet?" McAdams focused on that word.

McAdams watched Doctor Rosenburg nod to the man in the fatigues, the one he called Dell Ragnarsson. The man approached them, the fearful laser rifle slung over his right shoulder. He was a tall man, muscular, with short red beard and long strawberry blonde hair. His eyes were a piercing blue color. He moved with grace. McAdams instinctively knew that this Ragnarsson was a killer. She felt instinctively that he had killed before. It was in his eyes, he had the look of a predator.

McAdams was more correct in her observation of Dell Ragnarsson than she could ever know. He had been a soldier at one time before he learned that the real money to be earned was as a mercenary or a hired assassin. Ragnarsson had been hired by the Rosenburg family several times over the years to perform tasks such as kidnaping individuals or killing them. He gained no pleasure in his job. If there was a contract given to him that paid, he would take the job. The mercenary had accumulated a small fortune in selling his skills to others over the years. He had taken on many wives and produced dozens of offspring. Some of his children he took from the women he had bred with to raise on his own. Others, he left with their mothers and kept informed as to their progress from a distance. The children Ragnarsson took were trained by him to follow in his footsteps to become assassins themselves.

"When we found you on Earth, David Rosenburg selected you at the night club, my daughter and I drugged you." Ragnarsson told McAdams. "We put you into our space craft and then immediately into cryo-sleep. It took us about a month and a half to arrive here on planet New Edinburgh. You were brought to this facility on the Rosenburg Ranch Territory to become a member of one of the most influential families in all of the human empire. I am certain that you are aware that the Rosenburg's are members of the Royal Family. Vladimir Sikorsky, the Glorious Leader, is the grand-father of the man whose sperm was used to impregnate you."

McAdams wanted to scream, thinking that might wake her up from what she believed to be her worst nightmare. New Edinburgh was known on Earth as the dinosaur planet, some called it the purple planet. McAdams had read the news reports of the colonization efforts on planet New Edinburgh. She had seen the live broadcast feeds of the terrible reptilian looking monsters attacking soldiers and killing them. Thousands of humans had been eaten alive by creatures similar to the ancient dinosaurs of Earth. McAdams had read about the Dinosaur Wars as well, in which the military of the United Nations Space Command had pushed the prehistoric looking creatures away just long enough to establish cities and perimeters for humanity to begin to take over the northern continent of the newly discovered world.

"You understand that if you try to escape from here, you would be in danger of being hunted and killed by the population of meat eating life forms on this world?" Ragnarsson tried to impress upon the woman the cold facts of her situation. "You are safe so long as you remain within the walls of this Ranch. We are in complete control here and can protect you as long as you do not climb over the walls. You have no choice but to embrace this change in your life and become a Rosenburg. If you leave this province known as Rosenburg's Ranch, we will not be able to save you from the certain death that will find you on the surface of the planet. Do you understand me?"

"Yes," McAdams responded weakly. She was livid that these men had done this to her, without her consent. She quickly assessed her current situation. She was without friends, surrounded by committed hired thugs that do the bidding of their employer or father without question. McAdams would have to be smart and bide her time. She decided to play along with these madmen until she could devise a plan to escape and go home to her parents. Back to planet Earth.

McAdams closed her eyes and slept. She was not certain for how many days or hours. When she woke up, she was assisted into a wheelchair and taken from her hospital room to the outdoors. The first thing she noticed was that the sky was a red-orange color that was so bright that she was forced to shield her eyes by putting her hands over them. She could hear a sound off in the distance of strong winds and tried to turn her head and look behind her which caused a throbbing pain her neck. The man behind her, pushing the wheel chair told her that there was a dust storm in the distance. He explained that the planet of New Edinburgh had a unique climatology. The dust storms were so powerful that even the best space craft could be thrown off course by one. He compared the dust storms on New Edinburgh to the hurricanes of Earth with the exception the dust storms were on the dry land. He went on to tell her that the lightning storms were even worse. The electrical blasts would strike metal, as if it were attracted to it. A human being hit by a New Edinburgh lightning bolt would generally be dead upon impact, if they were so lucky.

McAdams found herself being pushed toward what was clearly a mansion of epic proportions. It was at least twelve floors high with marble streets in the front, surrounded by Doric columns and fifty marble steps leading to the entrance which was a double metal door. There were armed guards, in green uniforms and sporting laser rifles in their hands, walking on the rooftop and on the grounds. There were many other men and women walking the grounds, most of them wearing thick sunglasses to protect their eyes from the glare and one piece long sleeved suits of varying colors. There were hundreds, perhaps thousands, of people living either in the mansion or nearby. Most of them seemed to be unarmed. She noticed one of the men near her that was very tall with a muscular physique. He was the other man that had kidnaped her with Ragnarsson. She deduced he had to be the one named David Rosenburg. He winked at her when he noticed that she was staring at him.

McAdams was taken into a large den area on the first floor of the mansion. She counted eleven other women in wheel chairs that were present. Ten were clearly pregnant like McAdams and one woman was not. Of the eleven women McAdams saw, two were Asian, one was middle-eastern, one looked to be of Indian descent, four were white, one was Hispanic and two were black. Each of the women were absolutely beautiful. They all shared the same look of despair on their faces. McAdams knew exactly how each of them felt.

There were also two men holding serving trays with glasses on them. Clearly these two men were servants of some sort. They seemed happy due to the smiles on their faces. They were wearing matching white tuxedos with black shoes and black bow ties. McAdams deduced these two men knew exactly what to do, who to serve and when to offer that service.

The den area had a thirty foot high ceiling and two stair cases from the east and west of the room. There was a balcony that went all around at the point where the staircases connected. The walls were adorned with the heads of large reptilian creatures, mounted for show. In one corner was a stuffed silver and black furred four legged furry cat like creature. It had fangs, menacing eyes and was seven feet long and four feet high. McAdams was studying the shape of the stuffed animal when she heard several sets of footsteps walking down the west staircase. She looked up to see the man named Ragnarsson, wearing his green uniform and had his laser rifle slung over his shoulder. He had a web belt which had three throwing knives attached to it and a laser pistol. Walking with Ragnarsson were two uniformed and armed women. There was a man in a gold bath robe and slippers standing in between Ragnarsson and the armed women. The man in the bathrobe looked young and stood in between the two women while Ragnarsson stood at the top of the staircase, watching everyone with sharp concentration.

The man in the center of the two women seemed important and McAdams noted that his clothing that would cost thousands of Empire Dollars. His hair was perfect, not one strand out of place. He walked with ease and grace. Before he said his name, McAdams instinctively knew who he was.

"I am Alfred Rosenburg, the Second," the man announced proudly to the women. "You were all selected for the privilege of giving birth to my children. You do not have to thank me for selecting you for the honor. All I ask in return is that each of you worship me as if I were a God. Because I am a God! I am over one hundred fifty years old and I will never die." He reached the last step of the stair case. "You see, my family has discovered the way to live forever. And that gift will be given to each of you lovely ladies as long as you agree, today, to continue to produce offspring for me and my sons over the next decade. Give us ten years of producing children and we will give you eternal life in return."

Rosenburg paused and waited for one of the men in the white tuxedo's to bring him his morning glass of lemon tea. The man walked over to his master and kneeled before Rosenburg and held a red glass up to him. Rosenburg took the glass and sipped from it. The women watched Rosenburg savor the flavor of the tea.

"Perfect," Rosenburg said after a short pause. "Please, serve the women." The two men in the tuxedos began giving each of the women a glass of lemon tea each. Rosenburg waited patiently until all of the pregnant women had the cold drink in their hands.

"Now!" Rosenburg clapped his hands together. "This is the arrangement. Each of you will give birth to my children within the month. Then, you will be selected randomly to either give birth to more children for me, or you will breed with one of my sons. You met my son Cush at the medical facility. He is handsome. He will choose one of you and his selection will share his bed and produce offspring for him. You will be honored to do so if you are fortunate enough to be selected by him.

"To give birth to children for our family is the greatest gift any woman can receive in the universe." Rosenburg pointed to the sky and turned in circles. "Most of you, before you were brought here, never even considered what your legacy would be in the galaxy. I bet that none of you ever thought to ask questions such as what am I here for, what will my life be. Did you ever wonder what your purpose in this universe would be? Well, your destiny has found you. Now, you will give birth to Gods among mankind. Your children will grow up to become great leaders. They will be managers of great manufacturing concerns, Generals, Admirals, explorers, and leaders in the United Nations. You do not have to applaud or thank me for bringing direction to your lives. Please. I know how much pride is in each of your hearts that you are now here."

McAdams looked at the other women in the room. Some had the look of disgust on their faces, others despair. None of the women were smiling.

McAdams was breathing heavily as her anger was rising with each word out of Rosenburg's mouth. She finally decided to speak up. "You are fucking insane!" McAdams screamed as she threw her glass of tea at Rosenburg. She observed in awe as Ragnarsson, in one swift motion, drew a large knife from his utility belt and threw it at the glass. The knife hit the glass dead center, shattering it in mid-air. As the broken glass, ice and liquid landed on the tiled floor the two men in the tuxedos ran to McAdams and grabbed her arms.

McAdams was cursing them all, even the other women for not resisting. She was struggling with the men that were restraining her. "What the fuck is wrong with all of you? These people are insane! Let me go! Damn it! I have a family back in Chicago! I have to get back to them!"

Rosenburg approached her and looked her in the eyes, "My poor dear. I am so sorry you do not see the special offering before you. Since you have refused, I will only allow you to deliver the three children you are now pregnant with. After your birthing function has been completed, you will be married off to one of my slaves as punishment. If you displease the slave that chooses you, then my justice will be swift and no mercy will be shown to you. You will die a horrible death. Do you understand me?"

McAdams spit in Rosenburg's face. He snarled and slapped McAdams across her right cheek. Rosenburg despised lower class humans, especially those that were prone to showing such disrespect to him and the fact that one of them had the audacity to spit on him was unforgivable. McAdams face stung from the impact. Rosenburg took a napkin from his coat pocket and wiped his face and turned his attention to the other women. "Do the rest of you feel the same way? Is there anyone else here that will reject my generosity?"

None of the other women spoke up as they were all too terrified to defend themselves. A few looked down at the floor in shame.

More uniformed soldiers came into the room and took hold of McAdams' arms. They dragged her from the mansion as she screamed and cursed the Rosenburg's. McAdams was soon back in her hospital room, her arms and legs were quickly strapped onto a metal bed and she was injected with a drug by a nurse. McAdams screamed and cursed until the drug caused her to pass out. She remembered little of the next month. The drugs that the medical staff gave to her kept her sedated and most of the time she was unconscious.

One morning, McAdams woke up and stretched out, yawning. She immediately knew something was different. She was not drugged to the extent she had been in the past. She could focus on things better than before. She reached down to her stomach and found she was no longer pregnant.

"Doctor?" McAdams called out. "Doctor?"

Doctor Matthew Rosenburg approached her, "Yes,? What can I do for you?" He was just as handsome as the other Rosenburg Doctor named Cush. His eyes seemed to show compassion for others as did the tone of his voice. He was different from the others she had encountered since arriving on the Ranch.

"Who are you?" McAdams asked, still delirious. "Where is the other Doctor?"

"My brother Cush is delivering babies as we speak. I am Matthew Rosenburg."

"The babies?" McAdams asked. "What happened to them?"

"We induced labor while you were under the influence of some of our drugs," Matthew explained calmly. "You gave birth to three very healthy children."

"Where are my babies?" McAdams realized that her maternal instincts were strong. She wanted to see them, to hold them, to smell them and look into their eyes.

Matthew stood up and began walking to the door, "It is unfortunate you rejected my father's offer. Had you accepted, you would be holding your two sons and daughter right now as we speak. It is so sad. My brother Robert had taken a liking to you. He would have been a wonderful partner to you. It is your loss."

"Where are my babies?" McAdams screamed at him. She began thinking that this was all a nightmare and that soon she would wake up. But the horror story continued for her.

"You will never be allowed to see them," Matthew calmly told her. "You will be married to one of the slaves and you will live out your years as a slave. We all had such high hopes for you. I am so sorry."

The doctor turned and walked out of the hospital room, leaving behind a screaming McAdams.

So there she found herself, in a room being selected by a slave named Carlton Rand to serve as his wife. McAdams was lifted to her feet and escorted outside to find her future husband, Carlton Rand, sitting on the back of some animal that resembled a horse from Earth, but it was different. This horse had four deep red eyes and six legs. The horse had a coat of fur colored deep purple and it had fangs. McAdams was taken aback by the sight of the beast.

"Do not worry," Carlton Rand told her as he held out his arm for her to take so she could join him on the creature. "I trained him. He will not attack you."

McAdams looked around her for any place that she could run to. There were guards with laser rifles everywhere, on the roof tops of the tallest buildings and she could see that there were more soldiers on the large walls around the Ranch. McAdams correctly concluded that if she were to escape and get back to Earth, today was not the day to make the attempt. She took Rand's arm and he lifter her up onto the animal's back.

McAdams heard the creature make a loud roar, much different than how a horse would speak. "What is she called?"

Rand said something in a language McAdams had never heard before and the horse-like creature began walking. "Her name is Lena. She is from Sikorsky's Planet. She was one of the Larianette's, a war horse for the Akarzdamedians. I train them for the Rosenburg's."

FORBIDDEN REGION

"Lena," McAdams said to herself. She thought that was a beautiful name. They rode for about an hour on the back of Lena before they arrived at the slave quarters. As they rode the graceful Lena, Rand told McAdams of the war in which humanity conquered Akarzdamedia. The Akarzdamedians attacked earth first, centuries ago and they wiped out the majority of the population on the continent of Africa and the nations in the Middle East. The alien invaders took over several strategic locations on Earth and began to force humanity to accept subjugation. The United Nations Security Council declared war due to the cowardly sneak attack of this alien race. All seemed lost to humanity until a small group of heroes from different nation states and different backgrounds joined together to defeat the common enemy. Led by Vladimir Sikorsky, his oldest son named Vladimir, II, Robert Andrews and his children, the family known as DeMartino, the family named Brey and many others, humanity fought back. They first took over the alien bases on Earth and captured the Akarzdamedian space ships. The war lasted a decade, ending when the Earth Empire had enough war ships to subjugate all of the planets in the solar system of the Akarzdamedians. Earth used nuclear weapons, vaporizing most of the enemy. The surviving Akarzdamedians were forced to capitulate.

"There are several hundred Akarzdamedians here, on Rosenburg's Ranch, that are slaves just like me," Rand told her. "I will let you meet them some day."

"What do they look like?" McAdams wanted to know.

"Like giant cats that walk upright on their hind legs. They vary in color of skin and have no tails like cats on Earth. They have larger eyes than us and are thinner. But they are several times stronger and they are very intelligent."

There were hundreds of men, women and children living in the ninety buildings that McAdams observed. Each of the slave buildings were log cabin style and colored a bright pink. McAdams observed several statues of the Glorious Leader and smaller statues of the heroes of the Inter-Planetary Racial War against the Akarzdamedians. As a young girl, McAdams had idolized the long dead hero named Judy Andrews, who had served on a science vessel named Calypso during that war of almost two hundred years ago. Her father, Robert Andrews, had been the Captain of the Calypso. According to the historical records, Judy Andrews had been sixteen at the time of the war and for the past two centuries had served as an example to teens on how to serve the Glorious Leader. The Calypso perished in the final battle of the war when the humans were able to defeat the Akarzdamedians on their home planet. McAdams smiled to herself when she saw the life size statue of Judy Andrews as it reminded her of her happy childhood.

"The wood on New Edinburgh is the color of the ancient zebra wood on the desert continent of Africa on Earth," Rand explained to her. "We live in this home to the left." He was pointing to a log cabin that looked to be about two thousand square feet.

McAdams swallowed hard as she looked for any useful machinery that she might use in an escape attempt. There were no space ships that she could observe in the area. Nothing that she could see that would aid her in her mission to get her three children, steal a transport and get back to Earth. Her plans to return home would never work if she acted alone. McAdams realized she needed an ally and there could be no better ally than a loyal husband. She decided to be the dutiful and loving wife to this Carlton Rand and when she felt the time had come, she would enlist his aid in her escape.

The next year passed by and McAdams found it easy to be the good wife to Rand. He was always kind and loving to her and never said a negative word. He was also passionate in the bedroom. He had some stature in the community, they were well fed for their labors. They had everything a loving couple could want, except for their freedom. McAdams missed her family on Earth terribly and she also longed to see her children that were in the control of the evil Rosenburg's. McAdams would sometimes daydream about how her three children looked and wondered whether they would love her if she found them. Would she be able to kidnap them and escape? She tried to put such thoughts out of her mind.

One night, after making love to her husband, McAdams decided it was time to test her husband.

"Carlton, I need to get home, to Earth."

Rand was running his fingers gently through her hair. "We cannot leave my love. Our life is here to work the ranch."

"But my life before I met you was on Earth," McAdams said sadly. "I have parents, siblings. I must get back to them."

Rand shook his head, "Impossible. The only way out is in the Forbidden Regions. There are hundreds of dangerous creatures there and we would be dead before we got ten yards from the protective walls of the Ranch. We have a good life here."

McAdams kept insisting, night after night, that they attempt an escape. Rand kept telling her no. But what McAdams did not know was that because Rand loved her completely, he began scouting out the docking areas and formulated a scheme of his own to help his wife in her desires to go back to Earth. In his numerous trips to the landing strips and docking areas, Rand found that several ships seemed to be left unattended. He was able to steal a booklet on how to fly and operate one of the space craft. On another day, Rand was able to conceal two hand held laser pistols under his tunic. A week later, he took some hunting knives from a stable of animals that he had been training. He devised a plan for he and his wife to escape. He would tell his true love of his plan and do all he could to return her to Earth so that she could be with her family that she missed so much. The deep feelings Rand had developed for the McAdams woman were the most powerful he had ever known. She was everything to him.

One night, Rand told McAdams of his plan. They would ride Lena into the main city of the Rosenburg Ranch Province and they would have to stun some guards at the Main Landing Strip for space craft. They would steal something called a Raumschiff. He showed McAdams the booklet on the space craft so she could study how to operate it. They would fly the vessel back to Earth and to her family.

McAdams wept and hugged Rand. Over the past year McAdams also grew to love this man. She loved him even more at that moment.

The couple planned for the time to leave. They accumulated extra plastic food packets which when heated in special machines, would expand into meals that would feed two people for a week.

The day arrived for them to escape. Rand and McAdams took their weapons in leather pouches to hide them. They also took leather pouches of breads and freeze dried sausage sticks made from poggie meat. They had additional back packs for the plastic food packets so that they would have enough food for the yearlong space flight. That night, they mounted Lena and rode to the big city, slowly, so that they would attract little attention. McAdams and Rand left Lena at a stable. McAdams hugged the Larianette good bye. She realized she was crying since she would miss the war horse named Lena and it was painful to her that they could not take the loyal beast with them.

As she followed Rand to the landing strip area, McAdams saw a huge paved blue concrete area. It was longer than it was wide. There were numerous statues of the Glorious Leader and his children all along the sides of the landing strip, hundreds of them. There were two massive towers at the North and South of the strip. McAdams saw hundreds of space ships of different designs and different shapes. All of them were unattended. Rand led her to one of the ships that were called Raumschiff's.

The Raumschiff that Rand had selected was about seventy feet high and two hundred feet long. McAdams recalled the books that Rand had stolen for her to read. From those materials, she knew that the Raumschiff had three levels. The lower level had sleeping quarters, storage areas, the engine room and loading ramps. The second level was the command area which consisted of a computer room, a small command area and weapons room. There were also recreation rooms, kitchens and a small gymnasium on that second level. The top level was the pilot's section that generally had seats for two with a massive computer command dashboard and transparent metal to serve as windows. The transparent metal was strong enough to withstand a meteor shower and the direct blast of a laser rifle.

Rand spied two guards that were patrolling the landing strip. He drew one of the stolen laser pistols that he had hidden under his pull-over sweater, got down on his knees and waited, aiming in the direction that the guards were approaching. He fired on both of the guards when they got close enough. The two men collapsed to the ground without a sound. McAdams and Rand moved quickly and dragged the two men underneath another ship to avoid detection.

"Which one do we take, Carlton?" McAdams asked.

Rand pointed to the Raumschiff to the left. It was metallic in color and the back walking ramp was open and extended to the paved surface. "That one will get you home."

"Get us home," McAdams corrected him. "You are my husband and I love you. We go together. My parents and family will also love you. They are good people and we will have a good life together on Earth."

Rand kissed her. "I love you too. Let's go."

The two lovers ran to the ship. They saw the back bay door was opened and did not hesitate. They ran up the metal stairs. It was too easy, nobody was on board. They were home free. McAdams suddenly stopped in her tracks.

"Carlton," McAdams said softly. "My children. I need to get them."

He looked at her with disbelief, "There is no time. We have to leave now."

"I need them," McAdams pleaded. "Where would they be?"

Rand sighed, "They would be in the Rosenburg mansion. They are probably being raised by one of the other women that did not stand up to the family."

"What is the security like there?" McAdams asked.

"Guards everywhere," Rand shook his head. "We would never make it. They would kill both of us before we even got close to the mansion. I am sorry. But, this request, we cannot do it. It would be the end for both of us."

McAdams began to sob and sank to her knees. She longed to hold her children, to see them, how they looked. The pain for her was unbearable.

Rand hugged her, "When we are safe, we can bring attention down upon the Rosenburg family. We can get help from the people on Earth. Perhaps it is not hopeless."

McAdams nodded, knowing that she must leave now with this kind and decent man. "Let's get off of this planet."

As the lovers stood up she heard a yell. There were other security guards and they had found the two unconscious guards. Alarms sounded, the noise was like a loud siren. Rand pressed a button on the wall of the ship to retract the loading ramp and close the back doors. He ran to the stairs and urged McAdams to follow. They made it to the control section and then they climbed the ladder up to the pilot section. McAdams saw two black leather pilot seats and a long computer control panel that stretched from wall to wall. Rand jumped in one of the seats and began pressing buttons to initiate the launch and start the engines. McAdams realized Rand had memorized the instruction booklet in preparation for this day.

McAdams noticed that several men and women in green suits charging toward the airfield as Rand had the Raumschiff powered up to lift off. The people in the green suits were running at them from several different directions, brandishing large laser rifles in their hands.

"Those men!" McAdams pointed, her voice was shrill from fear. "They are coming right for us!"

Over the communication system on the Raumschiff came a voice. "Occupants of Raumschiff Rosenburg Number 7776, power down! You are not cleared for flight. That is a direct order."

The demand was repeated over and over. Rand looked for the weapons display. He realized that they would have to fight to escape. Rand located the targeting mechanism for the ship laser defense system and fired the laser canons at the guards charging at them. The laser bursts hit the men and women. McAdams gasped in horror as their bodies were blown to pieces. Chunks of meat, flesh and bone were all that was left, with smoke from the blast coming from the body parts. "I only meant to stun them," Rand said sadly, seeing that the laser blasts had killed the Rosenburg guards.

Rand quickly wrapped his hands around the half-moon steering column and began to pull it upward. The Raumschiff responded and lifted off, McAdams heart was racing as she watched them rising upwards through the transparent metal viewing windows. She could see the ground below shrinking as they ascended toward the sky. They were going to make it, she thought.

That was until she felt the Raumschiff sustain an explosion from the rear. They had risen about fifty feet in the air when a rocket hit them. There were warning sounds from the on board computer instructing them to brace for a crash landing. McAdams looked over at Rand who was struggling with the half-moon steering mechanism, gritting his teeth as the ship spiraled out of control. Despite his best efforts, Rand could not get the ship to respond. McAdams screamed as they crashed into a green field just four kilometers from the airfield.

Both Rand and McAdams were knocked unconscious by the impact.

McAdams woke up to find herself bound to a chair in an arena type setting. It was similar to the old Roman Coliseum with seating for thousands. There was no roof on this arena, and McAdams could see the red orange sky above. There was powdered purple sand covering the entire floor of the arena. On the arena floor level were four large gates, like prison bars, that were on the north, south, east and west sides. She could hear the roar of applause from the crowd of over three thousand people that were seated around the arena, waiting for the next death. McAdams saw that the purple sand had some spots that were wet from spilled blood.

She looked to her left and right and saw that Alfred Rosenburg the Second and Dell Ragnarsson were seated on either side of her.

"Good," Rosenburg said. "You are awake."

McAdams saw many people in the stands. Some of them were slaves that she and Rand had befriended over the year. They were cheering like maniacs as a man was forced out of one of the gates on the floor. McAdams squinted her eyes and recognized that the lone man was her true love, dressed only in a loin cloth. In the light purple colored dirt floor of the coliseum was Carlton Rand. He stood alone, listening to the sound of the howling mob.

Rosenburg stood behind a microphone that seemed to float in thin air. "Silence!" He demanded of the crowd and repeated the command several times. The screaming stopped. Rosenburg smiled as this was one of his favorite past times, to be a spectator at his arena and watch others die. He was clearly enjoying himself. "I am the kindest keeper in the entire Eight Solar Systems! I give love to all who serve me! So why, why would one of my beloved subjects kill some of my guards and try to steal one of my ships?"

Nobody answered until Rand himself screamed at the crowd. His voice echoed around the coliseum. "We wanted freedom!"

Rosenburg began laughing hysterically, clapping his hands together. "Freedom? That is such an over rated idea. Did I not clothe and feed you well? Did I not provide for you safe and clean housing? All of you watch now, the price of freedom. Open the gates!"

Rand was turning in circles as he heard the metal gates on the north, east, south and west of the huge coliseum opening. He saw one creature come out of each gate and roar. The other three also appeared from behind their gate. All four were the dreaded killer alligators from the Forbidden Region Great Lakes. All four were large scaly creatures, yellow skinned and large mouths with razor sharp fangs. They were a length of at least fifteen feet to twenty-five feet long from head to tail. The Great Lakes were in the southern most portion of the Northern Continent on New Edinburgh. The earlier settlers of the planet thought that building homes next to four large lakes would lend them a better chance at survival. There would be plenty of water, the ability to raise crops and tend to livestock. But, there were also these large creatures that came from the water to feed. They ate livestock, children, women and men. The large alligators were named "Great Lakes Crocs" due to their similarity with the alligators and crocodiles of Earth. The major noticeable difference was their yellow skin color. The second major difference was that the Great Lakes Crocs has longer legs and could run faster than the Earth versions.

The Rosenburg family sent in professional mercenaries years ago to the Great Lakes on a mission to stun and bring to Rosenburg's Ranch several Great Lakes Crocs. That mission had been successful and the creatures were used for moments like this one, to execute an undesirable and teach the masses a lesson at the same time.

The crowd went crazy as the Great Lakes Crocs began to walk out onto the arena floor. There were chants for blood, demands that the monster eat Rand.

McAdams turned to Rosenburg and Ragnarsson, with tears in her eyes. "Please, stop this! I will do anything you wish! Please do not kill him. He only did what I asked him to do! Please! Kill me instead!"

Rosenburg slapped McAdams hard across the face, leaving his hand print on her cheek. "You will watch him die, bitch! And, then, yes, you will do whatever I ask!" Rosenburg grabbed McAdams face with his left hand and yanked her by the hair with his right. He turned her head toward the arena floor and forced her to watch the scene as the four starving Great Lakes Crocs began charging Carlton Rand. McAdams sobbed as she heard Rand scream in terror. He was yelling into the stands for someone to help him. Rand tried to run to his right and he was able to sidestep the first large man-eater. But the one from the east caught Rand's right arm in its' massive jaws. Rand screamed in agony as the creature bit down into his flesh and bone. The crowd wailed with approval.

Another of the Great Lakes Crocs chomped on Rand's' left leg and was able to tear it free of his body. Rand screamed as the third alligator bit into his torso. Rand's last feelings before death was his rib cage being crushed by the massive jaws. The crowd cheered as the large creatures devoured Carlton Rand's body.

While the entire stadium was roaring with approval, McAdams was weeping. "Why?"

"Why?" Rosenburg could not believe the woman was so stupid to even ask such a question. "Because you slaves must be kept in line! You killed about a dozen of my elite guards! That cannot go unpunished!"

"Carlton," McAdams cried as she watched the last chunks of his carcass being swallowed by the monsters. Rand had been the only one on the Rosenburg Ranch to show McAdams any kindness at all and he did not deserve his cruel fate.

"Dell, take her to the organ doctors," Rosenburg said coldly. "Your body will be harvested. We will cut out your liver, your kidneys, your heart, your muscles, and any other portion of your body we deem useful and those parts will be used to keep my children young."

Ragnarsson and another guard grabbed McAdams by the arms and began dragging her away. The crowd was howling still as there were other executions to follow. Although it was futile, McAdams struggled with the men. Her emotional pain was great, but soon, when the surgeons cut out her organs without the benefit of any pain medication, Jenna Taylor McAdams would die in a manner that would rival what had just occurred to poor Carlton Rand.

Ragnarsson and the other guard dragged McAdams out of the stadium and threw her in the back of a small space craft. McAdams could do little to resist as her arms and legs were bound. She screamed at the men every obscenity she could think of. Her flight was over within ten minutes. The doors to the ship opened and several men in blue medical uniforms took McAdams forcefully by her arms and slammed her hard onto a metal gurney. The fall knocked the breath out of her. The medical doctors pushed her into a building she had never seen before. It was three floors high and the outside was all white. There was some rock landscaping around the front of the building. The doors slid open and the gurney she was on was pushed inside.

One of the doctors stabbed something into McAdams neck. She immediately felt herself unable to move. McAdams tried to scream but she could not. The only physical movement she could muster was to breath, and that alone was extremely difficult.

She was pushed down several dark corridors. She could tell that she was descending downward. The air in the place was cold and damp. There were old pipes in the hall way and one was dripping what seemed to be water onto the floor. Soon, McAdams found herself in a large room, all concrete from floor to ceiling, with medical instruments on tables and what appeared to be freezer units lined up around the walls. She was lifted up by Ragnarsson and two doctors and then placed on an operating table covered with white linens.

"The reason you cannot move is that the staff stuck a stun dart in your neck." Ragnarsson told McAdams. "In those freezers along the walls is where your internal organs and useable body parts will be stored for future use. What we cannot use will be fed to the pets."

McAdams tried to move and could not. Her muscles were paralyzed. There was a tall Doctor that injected McAdams with a hypodermic full of some blue liquid. She watched in horror as the doctors took out some scalpels. McAdams recognized Cush Rosenburg as one of the doctors. She felt the sharp pain as they cut open her stomach. She screamed louder than she ever thought possible for her. The pain was intense. She saw the men pulling items out of her body, showing no reaction to her screams.

Ragnarsson was laughing at her. "That was your liver," he was pointing at the body organ that one doctor was placing into a metallic looking bag. "There goes a kidney."

McAdams was breathing heavily and cried out as she felt the pain as they put a saw instrument on her chest and removed her breasts. Another doctor was using a metal instrument to force open her rib cage. McAdams began coughing blood as she heard and felt the splitting of her bones. She died seconds after Cush Rosenburg cut out her heart and showed it to her.

The last words McAdams heard were from Dell Ragnarsson. "Don't worry, your body will give several Rosenburg's another thirty or forty years of life. Now you know what Rosenburg meant by immortality."

The universe would not remember Jenna Taylor McAdams. Even her murderers would forget her name over time. Eventually her parents and family on Earth would give up any hope of finding her. Her three children would never know who their true mother was. They would be raised by another woman to become ruthless members of the Rosenburg clan. Such was the way of the Rosenburg family. McAdams was not to be the first victim of the family, nor would she be the last.

SECOND PROLOGUE

DARKTOBER

Thick bolts of lightning crackled in the skyline as the thunder clapped and the hail peppered the metal and concrete grounds of Clovis City. The storm had lasted for three straight days and the climatologists predicted that there would be two more days of the punishing weather for the citizens to endure. The majority of the civilians stayed inside their homes or sought refuge in some of the tall shelters, some of which had close to eighty floors from the ground level and several more underground levels. Children in the many orphan homes cuddled together as the ground shook with each clap of the loud thunder. The strong winds made it difficult for pedestrians to make their way to and from work. Many businesses were forced to shut down due to the lack of traffic. Each rumble of thunder seemed to predict the doom that was coming for several of the colonists of planet New Edinburgh. The date was five October, 2529, the year of Sikorsky.

Planet New Edinburgh had been a discovery of grand proportions. She was an earth like planet, with oceans, land, and breathable atmosphere, minerals both known and indigenous to the new planet, plentiful precious metals, comfortable gravitational pull and soil ready for farming. But she also harbored many dangers. The original settlers had to fight the indigenous monsters of the planet for their land. The wars had been costly in lives lost and took several years. The military was able to secure large portions of territory in the northern continent and the engineers constructed great walls around each of those territories to keep the large flesh-eating creatures out. Although the large monsters ate thousands of humans alive, the most dangerous predator on planet New Edinburgh was man himself.

Some of the highest ranking leaders of the planet were about to learn that lesson the hard way.

Brigadier General Charles Melton Alfredrick Ramsey the Seventh of the Security Council Marine Corps had made a life changing decision for himself, his family and the citizens of the planet. After careful consideration and reflection, he began to advocate that planet New Edinburgh should embrace the political idea of Separatism. It had been a much debated subject on other planets since Vladimir Sikorsky seized power and began conquering other solar systems. Several other leaders had previously taken the position that each individual planet should have separate laws from those handed down by the iron handed rule of Sikorsky. The thought was that Sikorsky lived on a faraway planet and that the laws that he forced upon the Eight Solar Systems might be good for Sikorsky's Planet, but were unworkable elsewhere. Ramsey educated himself as to the Separatist Movement and after careful consideration of the arguments on both sides of the issue, aligned himself with them. The danger to his personal safety was that free speech was not allowed under the laws of Sikorksy, that is, speech that abdicated cessation or separate rule for a lunar or planetary body.

Ramsey, being the veteran of several battles, the top graduate of his military Academy and holding several collegiate degrees, was an astute and pragmatic man. If he was to lead the people of New Edinburgh to become the first planet to successfully secede from the Sikorsky Regime, he had to have all of the military commanders that he served with on his side. He set out recruiting them, one by one. The military commanders possessed leadership qualities that the Sikorsky appointed spineless politicians lacked. They were also, for the most part, very experienced in combat situations while the politicians were corrupt and inept in the ways of motivating others.

Army Major General Jamie Ahra Li Clark commanded the ground forces of Clovis City and was the ranking officer on the planet. She was a no nonsense leader, following the Military Codes to the letter. She had grown weary of the rules forced upon them by the Sikorsky's and secretly harbored thoughts of leading the people of New Edinburgh to freedom and self-determination. Ramsey trusted her and sought her out first. He made veiled remarks to her so that his statements could not be interpreted as treasonous, in an effort to determine whether or not she was amenable to the ideas of the separatist movement. She responded in a positive manner and the two began to speak together on numerous occasions on the subject of cessation. Clark and Ramsey became allies and began to give speeches to the media outlets that were designed to get the imagination of the citizens working and to start considering the benefits should separation from the Sikorsky controlled Security Council became a reality.

Ramsey gave a speech in which he advocated for every citizen to have the right to bear arms. The crowd that surrounded him as he spoke listened to him intently, their eyes wide with wonder and impressed with his veracity. Humans had lost the right to carry weapons almost two hundred years earlier, by decree of Vladimir Sikorsky. The people began to question that law due to Ramsey's eloquent speech. After all, if one of the heroes of the Dinosaur Wars spoke openly about the subject, it had could not be treasonous.

Clark gave a speech on the idea that perhaps the forced orphanage on single mothers in the lower income brackets was wrong. She advocated that the laws allowing the Military Intelligence to seize newborns from their mothers simply because they were unwed and struggling financially were unjust. She similarly questioned, in a separate speech, the laws against birth control. The majority of the people found her words to be reasonable and full of sagacity.

Ramsey found that the public was receptive to the ideas. He wrote his most powerful speech next and it was the one that most likely led to the order to have him assassinated. Ramsey delved into the United Nations form of government that Sikorsky had forced on each planet. The Representatives of the General Assembly were elected regionally. But the General Assembly had little power at all. The smaller Security Council, which held the real power, was filled with individuals that were appointed by Sikorsky and his family. The Security Council members could be removed whenever the Sikorsky's decided. The message was clear, to serve on the Security Council one must do as Vladimir Sikorsky dictated or be replaced. Ramsey held several interviews with the local state controlled news media and advocated for free elections for the Security Council positions. His argument seemed to resonate with the people.

General Ramsey, in response to a growing crime spree in Clovis City, proposed that the Glorious Leader authorize an end the ban on civilians carrying lasers or other forms of firearms. Ramsey only sought to enable the defenseless civilians to be able to fight back against the criminals.

But the people were not the only ones moved by Ramsey's speech. Vladimir Sikorsky heard of the open criticism of his rule by Clark and Ramsey. He acted decisively and swiftly contacted his descendants that were in control of a large land mass on planet New Edinburgh known as Rosenburg's Ranch. Sikorsky directed the elder Rosenburg to dispatch assassination teams to silence Clark and Ramsey. Sikorsky was equally angered at Space Command Admiral Elaine La Cote Male Taile Casados for her recent refusal to follow direct orders to have her Planetary Defense Squadrons to shoot down a private transport ship that was leaving Space Station Cy-7. The transport was full of innocents and Casados told her superiors on Sikorsky's Planet that she would not kill fifty people to stop one accused criminal. When pressed to follow the order, Casados told the Glorious Leader to go somewhere warm and unforgiving. For that insolence, Sikorsky decreed that she too must die.

The lightning storm was perfect cover for the team of professionals that were paid to eliminate Clark, Casados and Ramsey. Although the citizens of Clovis City would call the day Dark October because of the black clouds in the sky, the reality was that the assassins were sent in months ago with the mandate to eliminate the ranking officers on planet New Edinburgh. Although the killers were successful, they left behind several innocent dead in the wake of the carnage brought on by their pursuit of the pay promised by the Rosenburg family. The day would also be remembered by the colonists as The Purge.

For many of the colonists of Clovis City, it seemed as if The Purge occurred yesterday. It was still fresh in the minds of many. The citizens only saw the end result of several days of attention to detail to make the killings a success. Dell Ragnarsson, Junior and Ella Ragnarsson spent hours planning the individual hits from their large mansions located on

Rosenburg's Ranch. When they felt that they were prepared to proceed, they contacted their grandfather, Felix, and informed him that the time to execute the mission had arrived. They brought in several other professionals to assist them on the mission. Their targets were considered high value, meaning that they were high ranking military officers, and would certainly attract the attention of the news media, Criminal Investigation Division and Military Intelligence branch. Their task was not easy. It would be difficult to eliminate the officers and then escape Clovis City after the fact. Their plan must be ironclad to ensure that each assassin would escape arrest from the local police who would be full of righteous indignation once the officers were killed.

Dell Ragnarsson, Junior, called Junior to avoid any confusion between him and his father, devised a plan to kill the officers and those closest to them. He brought in some of his closest confidants to prepare for the date that the officers would be killed. Nikko Xian was the first team member to arrive in Clovis City, dressed in business attire so that he could blend in with the other politicians, lawyers, business owners and civilian governmental employees that frequented the area that he would be visiting.

Nikko surveyed the large concrete court yards that surrounded the government buildings for the United Nations Tower, the military command facilities and the many court houses and surrounding rail stations. He noted that there were several hundred ten foot tall to thirty foot tall statues of Vladimir Sikorsky and other Royal Family members that surrounded the outer edges of the court yards. Nikko placed small tear drop sized cameras on the chests of the statues so that he could view from his temporary hotel room the exact times that the targets for the assassinations would show up for work each day. Experience had taught Nikko that people are creatures of habit. Most would arrive and depart from their employment at the same time, day in and day out. He spent hours placing the tiny cameras that changed color to match the background of the item it had been attached to. Nikko next visited the United Nations Tower and pretended to be a tourist as he placed more hidden cameras around the entryways of the General Assembly, the Security Council, some of the elevators lift entrances and facing the dozen sliding front entrances. Nikko moved on to the military areas and repeated the task. By the time he had completed his work, he had placed several hundred cameras.

Ella Ragnarsson had set up the computer surveillance equipment at her three bed and two bath spacious hotel room which was located a few blocks away from the United Nations Tower. She began eating a celery stick that she dipped in ranch dressing when she began to receive the signals from Nikko's cameras. As she programmed the computers to chart the times of arrival and departure of their targets, she began unpacking her large black suitcases which contained the weaponry that the hit team would use. She laid out several laser rifles, sniper laser rifles with laser and heat seeking sightings, laser pistols and knives of various sizes and shapes on one of the beds and pulled out vials of poisonous liquids and spread them out over a business table next to a dozen hyper dermic needles. She inventoried the radioactive, solar energy and lithium based cartridges for some of the laser weapons as she waited for the first sign of their targets to appear. She had a headset that she put on that had an ear piece for her left side of her head and a teardrop microphone that was an inch away from her lips. She smiled at the clear images on the computer screens of the courtyard and the government buildings.

"Good work, Nikko," Ella said softly into the microphone.

"You are very welcome," Nikko responded softly as he continued walking around the military buildings to finish his assignment.

Junior Ragnarsson had staked out the individual homes of Casados, Clark and Ramsey. He had taken along with him an assassin named Vinnie Montrose. Montrose had a shaved head and wore a blonde wig to conceal his identity. He was an expert in computer photography and had cased other locations in his past in preparation for a killing. Junior had relied on Montrose for those experiences as well as the fact that he was a good shot with a laser pistol and knew how to handle himself in a fight. The two men photographed the homes of the three high ranking officers in the military housing section of Clovis City. Each of the targets lived in three story homes so that their families could live in comfort and style. The Glorious Leader demanded that his military receive the best in everything so that the youth would be encouraged to either enlist or apply for acceptance to one of the Academies. Both men were dressed in dark blue sweats with tennis shoes and stayed behind the tree lines that surrounded the housing units as they snapped pictures of the homes with their small two inch wide cameras.

"What about the other officers?" Junior asked as they moved from the Clark home in the direction of one of the other residences.

"I checked them out as you asked. Colonel Gorski and Major Evart are on temporary duty training in Lynott's Land with General Tan and her brigades." Montrose spoke as he sent his photographs to an encrypted satellite mail account from his small camera. "Captain Frye is almost always around and we will have to deal with her. Colonel Lipinski is always guarding Clark, so we can take her when we hit Clark. Each of the officers has a group of young officers that are staff officers for their units. If they are around we will have to kill them all."

"Then let's hope that they are," Junior responded. "The bloodier the scene, the bigger the impact. I think we should kill Casados in her home and kill everyone we find there so that the news media will have a bloody mess to cover. She has seven children and her husband has nine from another marriage. The civilians will back off of their separatist thinking when they learn that the children will die for their sins."

Montrose stopped when he spied on the next home. He knelt down on one knee and began taking pictures of the doors, windows and security systems. "For what the Rosenburg's pay, I would gladly blow up a school full of kindergartners and sodomize their mothers."

Felix Ragnarsson arrived at Clovis City a few days after his grandchildren. He brought one of his sons, Sigurd, to serve as a long range sniper in case the plans of Junior and Ella went awry. Felix walked the length of the long concrete and metal court yard, passing the many multi-colored flowers, trees and statues of past heroes so that he could familiarize himself with the lay of the land. His first impression was that any altercation that was caused in the court yard would bring about the deaths of many innocent bystanders. Felix was loathe to such an idea. It was his opinion that it was unprofessional to kill anyone other than the mark. But the Glorious Leader, Vladimir Sikorsky, demanded a public spectacle complete with killing some of the targets out in the open for the people to witness. Felix would honor the demands of Sikorsky since it was even more important to satisfy the paying customer. Once he was satisfied that he had seen enough, Felix Ragnarsson went to meet his friends in the Security Council for an early dinner.

The next morning, at six a.m. sharp, the team of assassins met at a restaurant on the southern section of Clovis

City for breakfast. They sat at a corner table and made their final plans. Ella was given the chore of killing Ramsey. Junior and Montrose would eliminate Casados and her children. Felix, Sigurd, Philip Prescott and Nikko would kill Clark and her officers in the morning while they were on their way to work. Clark's assassination would give the Glorious Leader the spectacle that he demanded. There would be many witnesses and plenty of opportunities for collateral damage.

But that night the weather changed for the worst. The storm came and the assassins waited in their hotel rooms for the deadly thunder bolts to cease. They were all surprised by the news that the soldiers of Clovis City were working despite the challenges brought about by the weather. Clark took on the risk of being electrocuted to death by an errant lightning bolt and led her soldiers each morning to the United Nations Tower. Nikko was impressed by the lack of fear Clark displayed.

Junior Ragnarsson made a decision as the team leader and instructed them that they would strike their targets during the storm. If Clark had no fear, then neither should they. Junior ordered that the following morning, thunderstorm or not, they would finish their mission.

Dominic Andolini had always wanted to please his father and, like most teenagers, he believed the way to accomplish that was to follow in his footsteps. Dominic had no idea that by accompanying his father to work during the late evening of the fourth of October that he would become involved in an event that he kept to himself for several years. His father was a wealthy engineer that had designed and supervised the construction of the Great Protective Walls that enclosed Clovis City. The large fifty foot high wall, which was even higher at other points, was built for the purpose of keeping the deadly life forms that were indigenous to the planet away from the human population centers. But the storms that had been hammering hail and thunder down onto the city caused several alerts that there were from possible cracks or breaches in the wall. Dominic's father concluded that the alerts were all false alarms. But as a precaution, he decided to spend the next day or two at the United Nations Tower Engineering Control Center to monitor the Great Wall in case a breach did, in fact, occur. Dominic volunteered to go along with his father so that they could spend some quality time together. At three a.m., Dark October became a reality. Junior Ragnarsson and Montrose entered the residence of Space Command Admiral Elaine La Cote Male Taile Casados. The military officers that lived in the neighborhood were asleep and the dark skies, thick rain and hail, covered the tracks of the assassins as they swiftly moved toward the front entrance of the white mansion. Junior kept watch from behind one of the tall Doric columns in the front of the home as Montrose attached thin wires to the security system at the doorway. The three story mansion had a motion sensor security system, which Montrose disabled by splicing the system with a hand held computer. The alarm did not sound when they turned off the security protocols and opened the front doors. The only sound was from the thunder and the hail hitting the ground.

Casados, her husband, her children and several officers slept as Montrose and Junior prepared to take their lives. Montrose crept into the basement and found two female Space Command officers sleeping in a guest room. Montrose covered their mouths with one hand and slit their throats with the knife he held in the other and left them to bleed out on their beds. Junior found the oldest daughter of the Admiral, Kate, asleep in her room on the first floor. Junior had studied the dossiers of the entire family. Kate Casados was a cadet senior at the local Clovis Academy studying biochemistry. Junior slowly crept over her, placed his left hand over her mouth and smiled when her eyes fluttered open. She screamed into his hand as he brought his sharp twelve inch blade knife into her heart. Junior enjoyed how it felt when he stabbed his blade into a person. He especially loved the look in the eyes of his victims as they first struggled and then succumbed to their fate, realizing that they were going to die. She struggled for a few seconds before she passed. Her eyes were staring at the ceiling of her bedroom as a bolt of lightning brightened the room. Junior cleaned the blade on her bed sheets before moving on to the next bedroom.

One by one, Junior and Montrose cut the throats of the other children in the home. In one of the small bedrooms, there were twin girls sleeping in a bunk bed. Junior recognized them as teenage daughters of the Admiral. Junior slowly climbed the ladder to the bunk bed and straddled himself over the sleeping girl. He inspected her face as he readied his knife. She was beautiful and Junior almost felt sad that she had to die. He placed his left hand over her mouth and slit her throat from ear to ear. She bled out quickly.

He silently climbed down the ladder and turned his attention to the girl in the bottom bed. To his dismay, she was gone. He searched under the bed, opened the clothes closet and did not find her. He silently cursed to himself and deduced that she must have woken up when he climbed on top of the bed.

Junior quickly moved out into the hallway and found that Montrose was waiting, holding the escaped teen in his arms with his right hand covering her mouth. The girl was crying and shaking from fear.

Junior approached her slowly and whispered over the sound of the rolling thunder. "Now, now. Do not be afraid. Your siblings are waiting for you."

The girl looked at Junior as if he were crazy. She screamed into Montrose's hand as Junior thrust his knife into her chest. She was kicking instinctively as she felt her life blood leaving her body and dripping onto the floor. Within a few minutes she went limp and Montrose dropped her corpse onto the floor. The two killers nodded to each other which was their way to confirm that all of the target children had been eliminated. They looked at the staircase that was at the end of the hall and walked rapidly in that direction.

FORBIDDEN REGION

Their main target, Admiral Casados, was asleep on the third floor. The two men crept silently into her room. They could hear the crack of lightening outside as they stood over the husband and wife. In unison, Montrose and Junior hacked the Admiral and her husband to death. Space Command Admiral Elaine La Cote Male Taile Casados died when she bled out in the bed of her own home. Casados had been the commanding officer of the United Nations Space Command Fighter Group 7,933, located on Clovis City, planet New Edinburgh and the highest ranking pilot on the planet. She died without knowing that her children had been killed too. Her husband was able to get a cry out as he felt the second blow from the knife slash into his abdomen. He died, spitting up blood as he rolled off of his bed and collapsed onto the floor.

Brigadier General Ramsey had been the top ranking Marine on the planet. He was always the first officer to report for duty. Ella Ragnarsson had a surprise waiting for him. Thanks to the cameras planted by Nikko, Ella knew that Ramsey always took a cup of coffee from the break room before turning on his personal three dimensional computer to begin his day. Ella was able to gain access to the main military building by using the access codes that Nikko's cameras recorded as another top ranking officer used it to gain entry. Ella was dressed in a form fitting black outfit that was made of a special material to keep the rain from accumulating on her. When she walked into the tall building, not a drop of rain was on her. She had her face covered by the same material. Over her shoulder was a black back pack filled with weapons and poisons that she intended to use to complete her mission. Ella walked rapidly toward the break room and found the large office coffee machine. Looking over her shoulder to ensure that she was alone, Ella set her back pack on a table and unzipped it and removed a vial full of white liquid. She looked around to confirm that she was still alone as she pulled out a hyper dermic needle and drew a full dose of the poison. She turned sharply, walked to the automatic coffee machine and opened it. She injected the liquid into the filtered water that was in the back of the machine, ready to be used to brew coffee for all of the Marine officers that would report for duty that day.

She quickly gathered her belongings and walked rapidly toward Ramsey's office. She found that his door was opened and smiled. "Mighty convenient," she whispered to herself as she crossed the threshold of the doorway and danced into his room as if she were a ballet dancer. She began humming a piece from Wagner's Tristan and Isolde to herself as she searched his office for his coffee cups. Nikko's hidden cameras had detected that Ramsey collected coffee mugs from all of the locations that he had traveled during his career. He kept them in a black granite glass display located at the far right corner of his office. She pulled out her lock pick set from her back pack and began working on the lock to the display. She continued humming to herself as she opened the door. Wasting no time, she began squirting a small amount of the poison into each cup with the hyper dermic needle. When she had put a dash of the deadly liquid into each cup, she closed and locked the display.

Her next act was the trickiest. She took a small strip of transparent paper, about six inches long and three inches wide. She held it up to the window and the glow from a lightning bolt revealed the fingerprints on the paper. She carefully placed the paper onto the display which caused the fingerprints to be left on the glass. The prints were those of Ramsey's wife. Nikko had uncovered that the Ramsey's were experiencing marital difficulties so it would be the first act of law enforcement to investigate her when her beloved husband dropped dead after vomiting his intestines all over himself. The purpose behind framing Vera Ramsey was due to her position on the Security Council. Even though she had been experiencing problems in her marriage, she would predictably demand justice for the murder of her husband. If she were to be arrested, tried and convicted, then her demands would fall on deaf ears.

Finished with her mission, Ella quickly inventoried the contents of her back pack to ensure that every item was accounted for. Satisfied that she was not leaving behind any of her tools, Ella began walking for the exit to the building. She almost made it to the wide sliding doors without being detected.

"Freeze!" She heard the female voice behind her.

Ella cursed under her breath and turned slowly to see a female Marine with the rank of Sergeant First Class on shoulders of her Class C camouflage fatigue uniform. The woman had a laser pistol aimed at Ella's chest.

"Who the hell are you and how did you gain access to this facility?" The Marine demanded.

Ella noted that the woman did not have a quivering voice and her weapon was not shaking, indicating that her opponent was well trained, confident and not going to scare away.

"You got me," Ella said with a meek voice. "I came to drop off a gift for Major Evart. I am one of his wives. He gave me his access card and I decided that it would be nice for him to come back from his trip and have something nice waiting for him when he arrives."

The Marine grunted at the explanation and motioned with the laser pistol. "Take off the mask. I know all of Major Evart's wives. Show yourself. What is your name?"

"Frida." Ella recalled one of the names of the several wives of the Major. As her father drilled into her during the years of training, always be prepared for the unexpected.

The Marine smiled at the mention of the name and began to lower the laser pistol, dropping her guard. That was all the opening that Ella needed. She ran at full speed toward the Marine and kicked her in the chest with both feet. The Marine screamed and fell backwards from the impact. She rolled on the grey tiled floor as she struggled to keep her grip on her laser. Ella did not give the woman a chance to recover. While pulling out a pair of brass knuckles and running at her at the same time,

Ella pounced onto the Marine and began pounding her fist into her face. The brass knuckles smashed the nose and teeth of the unfortunate Marine as Ella delivered blow after blow. The Marine struggled until she fell unconscious from the barrage she suffered, her arms and legs going limp on the floor.

Ella looked around her and surveyed the hallway. Seeing no other soldiers in sight, Ella stood up and dragged the non-commissioned officer by her legs toward the front doors. As she pulled the woman out into the court yard, the rain and hail slammed down on both of them. Ella moved quickly to get the woman behind the building to the location of the garbage incinerators. She kept looking over her shoulders to make certain that she was not being followed or watched. As she arrived at the giant green colored garbage incinerators, Ella released the Marines feet. To her surprise, the Marine was awake, possibly invigorated by the cold rain in her face.

"Please!" The woman held her left hand up at Ella. "Please don't kill me. I have a husband. My children. Please."

Ella knelt down next to her and stroked her short hair. "I know. I know. I studied you, Sergeant First Class Eniananfa Chaszzell. I know the names of all of the men and women that work with you in your unit. I know the names of your children. I know everything about you."

"Who are you?" Chaszzell said as she spit blood and water from her mouth.

Ella moved quickly around the woman, locking her hands around her chin and the back of her skull. She began to twist her head to the right. Ella whispered into her ear, "For you, I am the angel of death."

Chaszzell tried to yell as she kicked her legs in vain and waived her arms at her assailant. She felt the bones in her neck beginning to snap and Ella twisted her head harder. Ella strained her muscles and metal reinforced bones to their limit as she pulled on the head. Ella smiled to herself as she heard the sound of the bone cracking. The neck broke as Ella twisted the head of the woman with enough force to finish her off. Ella unzipped her side pants pocket and pulled out a hand laser. She set the setting on low and aimed at the neck of the body. She used the laser beam to sever the head from the body. Ella kept a collection of heads and was proud to add the head of Chaszzell to her trophy case back at her mansion at the Rosenburg Ranch. The heads of her victims were reminders of her past successes and made great conversation pieces for other assassins that would visit her mansion. After the head was removed, Ella lifted the corpse up and tossed it into the incinerator. She placed the head in her back pack and jogged back to the safety of her hotel room.

Dawn came but the dark clouds and rain kept the sun from shining through. As was their routine, Army Major General Clark and her personal escorts, Colonel Lipinski, Captain Frye, Lieutenants Viniavante, Brodie and McMurray, left their homes to report to work. The five women and one man kept in shape by running the several miles distance from their residences to the military headquarters building. The six officers were dressed in their Class C fatigues and held their heads high as they breathed in the fresh air from the rain storm. The rain and hail fell around them as they moved their legs with precision and keeping up with one another. At the half way point, they were joined by a platoon of enlisted men and women, all dressed in their fatigues. Some were in the Army green, others in the Marine camouflage and the remainder in the solid black uniforms of the Military Intelligence Branch. Sigurd Ragnarsson was the first to see them as they came into the view of his snipers scope. He had positioned himself on the rooftop of the United Nations Tower with a mounted Allen Corporation SSKL-77 laser sniper rifle aimed at the western quadrant of the court yard. The scope was coated with a special liquid to keep the rain from obscuring his line of sight and enabled him to trace body heat through the thick rain. He was dressed in a black outfit, similar to the one that Ella had worn, and had a tear drop microphone and headphone set on. The headset was synchronized to the frequency being used by his fellow assassins on the ground. As he confirmed that General Clark was on her way he informed the others.

Felix Ragnarsson, Nikko and Prescott were in position on the north, south and east quadrants of the court yard respectively. They were dressed as Sigurd and Ella and each man had a laser rifle ready in their hands. The plan was to catch the close to fifty soldiers in a cross fire, killing the majority of them before they would have the opportunity to draw their own weapons and return fire. Junior and Montrose were waiting at the west end of the court yard to fire at the rear of the soldiers and to cut off any that tried to escape the ambush.

Clark and her soldiers had no idea what had hit them. Her last memory was waving at three nurses that were walking toward the hospital that was located just a few blocks from the United Nations Tower. One of the nurses was the wife of a close friend to Clark named Sean Collins. She wished her a good morning just before the shooting started.

Clark watched in horror as the head of Colonel Lipinski exploded, sending brain matter and skull fragments into the rain filled sky. Frye was cut in half by a laser blast before she could react. Several of the enlisted soldiers were being hit by shots fired at them by the unknown assassins. Clark fell backwards as she watched the torso of Lieutenant Brodie get hit twice, sending her legs and arms flying in different directions. Clark struggled to draw her own laser pistol as she heard the screams of the dying and the sound of the laser fire. She turned to her left to see that the wife of Sean Collins and the other two nurses were on the pavement, dead from the laser fire. Some of the soldiers tried to fire back, but they had already lost the battle.

Clark tried to focus and aim at a man in a strange black suit at the northern quadrant. She never had a chance to pull the trigger. From his rooftop vantage point, Sigurd had Clark in his laser sighting. He fired his laser sniper weapon before Clark could manage to get her shot off and his aim was on the mark. Clark's head ripped open like a dropped egg, her brains and skull spattering in several directions. Clark's headless corpse collapsed to the pavement as the remainder of her soldiers went down in the unmerciful barrage of laser fire. Not one of the soldiers survived the ambush.

Sigurd Ragnarsson fired his sniper rifle which launched a light red one inch radius ball of energy with each pull of the trigger. Each energy ball was propelled faster than a bullet from an old style sniper rifle. When the target was hit by the round of energy, their bodies would be obliterated. Most of the victims that Sigurd shot on the court yard left little evidence that they had ever existed. A few legs and arms were left behind; the rest was reduced to spattered flesh and bone.

Military Intelligence Staff Sergeant Mark Lund had been working late at the United Nations Tower that morning. He had taken a break from viewing the building security screens and looked out the observation window from his office on the fifth floor. He was shocked to see the carnage that was being committed on the court yard. He saw dozens of civilians and even more soldiers being ripped to pieces by the assassins. He counted several shooters on the ground and noted that there were shots coming from above. He quickly theorized that the shots from above would not be from a space craft as most pilots were unwilling to fly in the bad weather. Lund cursed as he quickly deduced that at least one of the killers was firing from the rooftop of the very building he was standing in. He quickly concluded that he could not offer any assistance to the victims on the ground, but he could apprehend one or more of the perpetrators. Lund pressed the security alarm on one of the computer panels on the eastern wall to alert the MI soldiers that were in their barracks near the main plaza and then dashed madly toward the escalators that were at the far end of the hallway. The building was over one hundred thirty floors high. With the help of the rapidly moving escalator stairs, Lund estimated he could reach the rooftop in four to five minutes. He ran as fast as he could and pulled out his Holo-com device to call for back up. He leaped over some of the steps as he cursed at the other Marine unit when they indicated that they did not want to go out in the bad weather.

Lund turned off his Holo-com and pulled out his laser pistol. He rounded the twenty-second floor and rushed to the next set of escalators. His biggest fear was that the killer on the roof would get past him. He pushed himself to move his legs faster. He was soon near the forty-ninth floor when he saw the tall man in the strange black suit carrying a long black leather rifle pouch over his shoulder. Lund slid to a halt on the foyer of the floor, aimed his laser pistol at the man and shouted: "Freeze!"

Sigurd Ragnarsson had left his spot on the roof when he was certain that Clark and her military entourage had been eliminated. He had packed up his sniper rifle and left the rooftop to escape to the safety of his hotel room. Although s skeleton crew was always present in the United Nations Building, Sigurd never once thought that he would be discovered. He stopped moving his feet when he heard the command and put his hands up.

"Drop the weapon!" Lund ordered as he kept the laser pistol trained on Sigurd and walked slowly toward him.

Sigurd complied and let the sniper rifle slide off of his shoulder and onto the black granite floor. He smiled at Lund and said, "You should not interfere. You really should let me go."

"You just helped kill about ninety people out there!" Lund grinded his teeth as he thought of the atrocity. "Get up against the wall and spread your legs!"

Sigurd looked over his shoulder and sized up Lund. He smiled at him and slowly moved toward the wall as he had been instructed. "I was sent by some very powerful people, Staff Sergeant. How much do you earn in a month? Three thousand Empire Dollars? Four thousand? If you let me go and never speak of our encounter to anyone, my employers will compensate you to the tune of fifty thousand dollars. That is much more than you earn in a year. What do you say? How about it?"

Lund watched as the man put his hands on the wall, "Fifty thousand would not be enough money to buy headstones for all of the innocent people you just killed. I am taking you into custody and interrogation. Fuck your money."

"One hundred thousand, then?" Sigurd upped the offer.

"No."

"Five hundred thousand?"

Lund placed the barrel of his laser pistol at the base of Sigurd's skull, "Your killing days are finished. You are under arrest."

Lund had assumed he was dealing with a man, albeit a man that was well trained as a marksman, but a man of flesh and bone. He had no idea that Sigurd Ragnarsson had been surgically altered to be superior to the average person. His leg and arm bones had been replaced with metallic bones and his muscles were enhanced by surgical advancements and steroids. His strength was ten times that of the average man. Sigurd could move three times faster than Lund. The non-commissioned officer did not realize what he was getting himself into.

Lund began to frisk Sigurd with his free hand as he heard shouts down the hallway. He recalled that one of the Clovis City engineers, a man named Andolini, had checked in earlier with one of his teen-age sons in tow, to work on some project or another. Lund saw out of the corner of his eye that the Andolini lad had left his father's office and was approaching them.

"What's going on?" Dominic Andolini asked as he walked toward them slowly, rubbing his eyes as if he had just woke up from a nap. He had accompanied his father to work the night before to learn more about what his job was. When he heard the shouting from down the hall, he told his father he would check to see what was going on.

"Stay back, kid!" Lund warned as he continued checking Sigurd for weapons.

Dominic watched in awe as Lund ran his hand down the leg of the man against the wall. Without warning, Sigurd twisted around, slapped the laser pistol from Lund's hands and shoved him to the floor. Lund groaned as his back slammed to the floor. Sigurd leaped into the air and planned on crushing Lund by landing on his chest. Lund narrowly avoided death by rolling out of harms way. The granite floor cracked upon the impact of Sigurd's metallic feet and legs. Lund rolled to his left for several feet before leaping back onto his feet. He desperately searched for his laser pistol as he moved. He stood up into a martial arts fighting position and faced Sigurd.

"You should have taken the money," Sigurd smiled as he began walking toward him. "Now I have to eliminate you."

Lund charged at Sigurd and delivered a crescent kick to his head. Sigurd grunted and moved to his right as he tried to regain his footing. Lund landed on his feet, and began hitting the man in the abdomen with a flurry of punches. Sigurd laughed and backhanded Lund across the face. Lund was knocked off of his feet and flew fifteen feet into the air, smashing into the ceiling and then landing on the granite floor with a thud.

Lund felt as if he had a broken rib or three as he tried to recover and push himself to his feet. He could hear the footsteps of Sigurd growing closer to him.

"Now you have to die," Sigurd said to him.

"Sir, he told you to freeze!" Dominic Andolini said with a raised voice.

"Don't worry punk. When I finish him, I will kill you next." Sigurd promised the boy.

"No, I don't think so. Freeze or I drop you," Dominic said with a steady voice.

Sigurd looked over at the young interloper and began laughing when he saw that the kid had found Lund's lost laser pistol.

"Ha! You are a civilian! I bet you don't even know how to fire one of those things!" The assassin momentarily forgot Lund and began walking toward Dominic. "Now you are going to die very painfully. I was going to be merciful, but now that you really pissed me off, I am going to make you scream for death."

Dominic took in a deep breath as he had been taught by his father, Colonel Gorski, Major Evart and his instructors at the Academy. He squeezed the trigger. The laser bolt hit Sigurd in the chest and he stopped his forward progress as the energy encircled him. To Dominic's chagrin, the killer did not fall down. He laughed.

Lund was on his knees and could not believe that a laser shot would not drop the man.

"You cannot harm me!" Sigurd yelled as he shook his head and began walking faster toward Dominic. "That was a good shot, though. In the dark, over forty feet between us and right in my chest. I am impressed. If things were different, I would take you with me and train you. But, the games are over."

Seeing that the stun blast had no effect on the man, Dominic set the weapon on the kill function as Sigurd rapidly closed the distance between them. Dominic took in a deep breath, slowly exhaled and fired.

The laser beam blew a hole in Sigurd's chest and opened a baseball size hole out of his upper back. Sigurd shrieked in rage and pain as he staggered backwards. He looked down at his chest in disbelief and looked back up at the kid that had shot him. "You little bastard! Now you really pissed me off!"

Dominic swallowed as Sigurd began to charge at him. Dominic did not panic; he took a deep breath and fired three shots in rapid succession. The first hit Sigurd in the abdomen, the second in the right shoulder and the third shot hit him right between the eyes. The top of Sigurd's head was vaporized as he flipped backwards. His body slammed to the floor. Seeing that the crazed man was no longer moving, Dominic lowered the laser pistol and held it next to his right leg. Lund was soon by Dominic's side, looking at him with admiration in his eyes. "Where did you learn to shoot like that?"

"I have good teachers," Dominic responded as he handed Lund his laser pistol. "I think I panicked and killed your prisoner. Sorry."

Lund shook his head, "Sorry? You just saved our lives."

"What is going on out there?" Dominic pointed toward the windows in an attempt to change the subject. Dominic had never killed a person before and he was emotionally numb from the experience. "I was asleep and heard you running up here. My dad thinks that something was wrong in the court yard."

"A lot of people died today kid and you just took out one of the assassins. Go back to your father and lock yourselves inside the office. I am going to get us some help. Go on."

"Yes sir," Dominic began walking back down the hallway toward the discarded sniper laser rifle. He knelt down over it and lifted the leather pouch into his hands. "If this is what I think it is then this guy has a lot of money. The sniper models like this are extremely valuable."

"Take it with you then," Lund said as he inspected the remains of Sigurd. He searched his clothes for any evidence of his identity.

"Really? You don't need it for evidence or stuff like that?"

"Kid, you did awesome," Lund complimented him. "This was a well-organized hit. Take the weapon, hide it and tell no one of your part in this. These are dangerous people and you just killed one of them. Take it home and forget this ever happened."

"What about the body?" Dominic motioned the barrel of the laser weapon in the direction of the corpse.

Lund pursed his lips, "I'll get rid of it. We are the only two that know what happened here. I will inform some of the officers, if any of them are still alive, and I will take the blame or credit for killing this fellow. These men were professional killers. If they learn about you then they will most certainly want to come looking for you because you killed this man. Keep a low profile. Got it?"

"Yes sir."

General Ramsey had been notified via Holo-com that there had been a massacre at the government buildings. He found that his disloyal wife was not in his bed as he checked the time. It was just after four a.m. He moved rapidly to his closet, found his military fatigues, dressed and moved to his personal transport that was waiting from him outside. He ran through the rain and hail to jump into the driver's seat of his baby blue four door automatic Brackenridge Corporation solar powered eight wheeled vehicle. He verbally instructed the vehicle computer to start the engine and for the automatic pilot to get him to the office.

The trip took about five minutes. Ramsey leaped out of his vehicle and was appalled at the carnage he viewed as he arrived at the scene. He estimated close to one hundred bodies were scattered around the court yard. Several dozen soldiers were roping off the crime scene and medical personnel had already arrived to see if any of the fallen could be saved. Ramsey walked out of the rain and into his office. As he walked, Corporal Nandy Plantard handed him a cup of freshly brewed coffee and followed him to his office.

"What happened?" Ramsey demanded as Plantard shut the door behind them. He turned and faced her, smiling. He was glad to see her there. They had been involved in an extra marital affair for the past several months, normally making love on his desk top.

She rushed into his arms and they kissed passionately. Ramsey ran his hands up and down her buttocks as he moved her toward his desk. As she sat on the desk top, Ramsey took a large gulp of the coffee and set the cup on the desk. He began to unzip the front of Plantard's uniform when he suddenly felt a stab of pain in his chest. He began to see bright flashes of light as he staggered sideways and grabbed the edge of his desk with one hand and grasped his chest with the other.

"What's wrong?" Plantard was alarmed as Ramsey struggled to stand. She stood up to help her lover, hoping that whatever was happening would not be serious.

Ramsey screamed as he fell to the floor on his hands and knees and began to go into convulsions. He was vomiting blood and his internal organs that were being reduced to liquid due to the acidic effects of the poison that had been planted by Ella Ragnarsson.

Plantard screamed as she heard other shouts of despair as many service men and women vomited their liquified internal organs onto the floor after drinking the coffee.

Ramsey died from the poison on the floor of his office. Seventeen other service men and women suffered the same fate from the poison in the coffee.

After a quick investigation led by Lund and some of his MI squad, Ramsey's widow was arrested and charged with multiple murder charges. As she was awaiting her day in court, she maintained her innocence.

Junior Ragnarsson had his team depart the city in separate transports. For the team of assassins, Dark October was completed successfully. Others later referred to it as The Purge or Darktober. In the aftermath, lower ranking military officers had to fill the command slots left open by the deaths of Casados, Clark and Ramsey.

Felix Ragnarsson returned to his mansion located on Lynott's Land while the rest of the assassin team safely returned to the Rosenburg Ranch Territory. After a few weeks time, Felix realized that his son, Sigurd, had never returned. Felix worried that his son had been captured, but there were never any news reports that substantiated his fears. He waited in vain for his son to contact him and despite his efforts to locate any clues as to his whereabouts, he never learned of his ultimate fate.

General Ramsey's brother was a financial director at a hospital and did not believe that his sister in law was the killer. He was constantly showing up at the United Nations legal office, without an appointment, making demands regarding the case. His constant interference with the murder investigation drove prosecutor Sean Collins to anger, especially when the older Ramsey would interrupt his day. What had never been discovered was the fact that General Ramsey had been assassinated by Ella Ragnarsson as she left behind no DNA or fingerprints. But the physical evidence connecting the widow to the murders was overwhelming. Collins and his staff of lawyers prosecuted Ramsey's widow and obtained multiple murder convictions against her. She was sentenced to seventeen separate ninety year sentences to be served on the prison planet Cootron.

Sean Collins mourned the death of his wife. Many other family members of the victims of Dark October did the same. Numerous funerals for the fallen were attended by hundreds. As the years passed, Clovis City grew in population and the people did their best to put the event behind them. Clovis City grew and housed thousands of thriving businesses, to include bars, restaurants, high tech retail outlets, large farms, private transport businesses, clothing manufacturers and mechanical repair locations. The military school, Clovis Academy, expanded over the next three years as enrollment increased. The New Edinburgh Marines Brigades was placed under the temporary command of Colonel Nikolai Gorski, the 10,888[th] Army Corp was placed under the command of Major Sigebert Evart, even though he was a Marine and the United Nations Space Command Fighter Group 7,933 was placed under the command of Space Command Captain Ana Rendon and transferred to the Dakota Province.

Gorski and Evart were among the first to inspect the crime scene at Admiral Casados' home. They were both moved by the butcher job done on all of the teens and children in the home. Gorski could not get the image of a seven year old boy that was impaled to one of the walls with a short sword. He thought of his two sons being killed in such a manner. He was certain that the killers were sending a message through their willingness to be so brutal. Clark, Casados and Ramsey had spoken out against the Glorious Leader and were killed for it. But their families and close friends were made to suffer the consequences as well. The hilt of the sword had two capitalized silver letters "VM" inscribed on the side.

"Message received," Gorski mumbled to himself as the police investigators pulled the boys corpse from the wall.

"What was that?" Evart asked, not hearing what Gorski had said.

"Nothing Sigebert. I was just talking to myself. Let's go home and check on our own families before we get knee deep into this investigation."

Evart nodded in agreement as the investigators slid the young Casados into a body bag. "So we are looking for a man or woman with the initials VM? Not much to go on."

Gorski stepped over a pool of blood on the floor and looked up and down the hallway. "I doubt that whoever left that even goes by those initials anymore. This was a well-planned hit. We will never find the people that did this."

Over the years following Dark October, the population of planet New Edinburgh grew as new immigrants from other planets arrived to settle in one of the eleven provinces. The new arrivals required additional services which meant that the government had to expand as well. The Andolini Engineering Company was contracted to build on to the existing United Nations Building. After eight months of work the building went from a single tall building to a series of buildings. The United Nations Tower itself, also known as the Administration Building was one hundred thirty seven stories high and had been expanded into three wings, almost like the shape of a capital "M." The redesigned building consisted of a huge hall for the General Assembly of the United Provinces of New Edinburgh.

Each of the eleven provinces sent an Ambassador that was selected by Vladimir Sikorsky to vote on all policy recommendations that were to be sent for approval to the United Nations of Earth on Sikorsky's Planet. The General Assembly of New Edinburgh selected a Secretary General every four years from their membership. Each of the eleven Ambassadors served four a term of four years and were given a large support staff with offices in the same building. The Secretary General personally appointed the five members of the Security Council.

FORBIDDEN REGION

The UN Tower also housed the Judiciary for the entire planetary system. The Judges were selected to life terms by the General Assembly. There were several criminal courts and civil courts in the building that heard arguments from lawyers and testimony from witnesses. On any given day, one could find magistrates that were selected to serve in the eleven regions, the lunar base and Space Station Cy-7 to dispense with local issues. There were many offices delegated to lawyers to advise the Secretary General and the General Assembly and more lawyers that prosecuted the criminal cases for New Edinburgh. There were even more lawyers that had specific board certifications in areas such as property law, mineral law, oil and gas law, administrative law, the law of astral navigation and military justice that served as advisors to the lawmakers. Each of the judges had offices with support staff including clerks, court reporters, computer technicians, body guards, drivers, and budgeting analysts. The lawyers also had offices allocated for secretarial staff, research assistants, legal assistants, runners, clerks, some body guards and drivers.

In addition, the Tower had another large hall for the New Edinburgh Security Council, which handled issues of Planetary Security, in other words, the defense of the colonies. Only five of the eleven provinces had seats on the Security Council. Those provinces were the most influential on the planet and housed members of the Royal Family, and those individuals ruthlessly controlled those territories. They were the Rosenburg's Ranch,

Clovis City, Lynott's Land, Gellar's Province and Murdock's Province. Those five provinces submitted candidates for the Secretary General to select from. Those five members served for six year terms. Each of the Representatives of the Security Council had large support staff as well. The Secretary General possessed the largest support staff of all.

Before and after Dark October, the Secretary General of the New Edinburgh Security Council was Alexander Lyss. He was in his second term for that position. He had come from the Rosenburg Ranch Province where he had retired after serving in the Military Intelligence as an officer. Unknown to the majority of the citizens, it was Lyss that had given access to the governmental buildings to the assassins. Lyss was as corrupt as a man could be, accepting pay offs from the Rosenburg family in return for giving them favors whenever they asked. He was fifty-eight years old, had four wives and fathered seventeen children. One of his wives was a Rosenburg which made his selection to the powerful post almost inevitable. When New Edinburgh was being settled by humanity on its' Northern Continent, Lyss accepted an offer from the Rosenburg Corporation to live on the Rosenburg Ranch property and serve in the General Assembly. During the so-called Dinosaur Wars, Lyss was able to gain a position on the Security Council and was later appointed the Secretary General. Lyss proved to be a capable administrator during the infamous Dinosaur Wars. He had to overcome many challenges during the conquest of the Northern Continent and handled each crisis with competence. Politically, he was the most influential man on the planet.

After the Dark October assassinations, Lyss was forced to rely on three men and one woman for advice on legal, military and administrative issues. The first was his legal advisor, Sean Collins, II. Collins was forty-seven years old and a very accomplished trial lawyer. Collins had started his legal career as a military lawyer in the Space Command, prosecuting soldiers in the military courts. He served five years and then went into private practice and had litigated hundreds of cases, earning a stellar reputation in the court room. Based on his record of success, Collins was hired by the General Assembly of New Edinburgh to be chief counsel. When Lyss rose to power, he had Collins become his managing attorney. Lyss placed Collins was in charge of all of the legal management for the planet of New Edinburgh and allowed him to prosecute the high profile criminals. Collins had been married twice. His first wife had reportedly committed suicide. Collins remarried many years later only to lose his second wife during Dark October. Collins had many children and relied on a live in employee to assist him in the daily house work. Three of his children were students at the Clovis Academy and another had graduated. The oldest daughter, named Ginger, recently married another cadet. Lyss was honored when he was asked to conduct the wedding ceremony by Collins.

Lyss reluctantly relied heavily on Colonel Nikolai Gorski, the highest ranking Marine Corps officer on the planet. Colonel Gorski arrived to New Edinburgh as a young Lieutenant. His wife had died before landing on the planet and the Colonel never remarried. Gorski had two sons, one was attending the Clovis Academy and the youngest son was enrolled at the Preparatory School on Clovis City. Colonel Gorski had obtained several medals and promotions due to his fierce leadership in the Dinosaur Wars. Gorski almost died in several battles, and had a large scar on the left side of his face due to a claw slash from one of the deadly monsters he had fought. He almost lost his eye in the attack. Gorski also lost his left arm in another dinosaur attack and had a metal arm made of several alloys including tungsten, nickel, iron and molybdenum, covered by a synthetic flesh and flesh hybrid. Gorski had grown as a close friend to Lyss, Collins, retired Admiral Seward and Major Sigebert Evart over the many years.

Lyss also kept the company and counsel of Major Sigebert Evart. Evart was a tall man, standing at six foot six inches. He was married to multiple wives and had fourteen children, all girls, which was the subject of much of his morning conversations around the break room. He was a proud father and bragged constantly about his girls. Evart was loyal to Gorski and the other Marines under his command. He was a brilliant tactician and had a working knowledge of engineering. Evart had two nephews at the Academy, Michel and Flora Evart.

FORBIDDEN REGION

Gorski and Evart had become the de facto military commanders of the planet when the Generals on New Edinburgh were assassinated. General Tan should have been the officer in charge but she rejected the responsibility as she preferred to remain on her seat of power in Lynott's Land. Lyss was terrified of Tan as she had a reputation for an explosive personality, almost bi-polar in the way she conducted herself. One moment Tan would be your best friend, the next she would be shooting you in the back of the head. Lyss was wary of Gorski and Evart, but preferred dealing with the two men over Tan.

Lyss had been an asset to the assassins when all of the officers were eliminated by the Rosenburg family on Dark October. Lyss worked closely with the killers and had even recommended the killings. He had been privy to meetings in which Clark and Casados were preparing to send in expeditions to the Rosenburg Ranch to investigate claims of slave trading and manufacturing of untested weaponry. Lyss informed the Rosenburg family of these actions. So, they sent in the best assassins that money could buy, the Ragnarsson's, and they killed all of the top officers. Framing one of the widows for Ramsey's death and making the other killings a bloody spectacle, was just icing on the cake.

Lyss had been waiting for the replacement Generals to arrive, but it had been some time. Gorski was the highest ranking officer in Clovis City for now and Lyss was satisfied with his performance. The only officer alive on planet New Edinburgh that out ranked Gorski was General Leta Tan from Military Intelligence. Tan despised the daily management and politics of the United Nations so she isolated herself on Lynott's Land and ran her brigades from that location. Tan was in her forties and had a reputation for being cruel and decisive in delivering punishment. She had killed dozens of accused by her own hand.

The last confidant of Lyss was Rebecca Rosenburg, one of the daughters of Alfred Rosenburg the second. Rebecca was twenty-five years old, single and very attractive. She had long dark hair, blue eyes, striking facial features and she was well educated. Rebecca had been hired by Lyss when she was twenty-two years old to be his executive assistant as a favor to her family. Lyss was glad he had hired her. She was a smart lady and assisted him in the day to day management of the finances of the Secretary General position. The fact that she was sleeping with him on the side was a fringe benefit that he had not expected when he hired her.

Colonel Nikolai Gorski had returned to Clovis City the moment he learned of the purge of the two Generals and the Admiral. He found that the people seemed to be living in fear since the killers had not been apprehended. Gorski directed his top criminal investigators to make solving the murders their first priority. After over three years, the investigation had resulted in no arrests. The only clue was the body of Sigurd Ragnarsson that was delivered to Gorski by Lund. Gorski promoted Lund and assigned him to be the Non-Commissioned Officer in Charge, also referred to as the NCOIC, of the undercover Military Intelligence platoon in Clovis City. Lund also searched for clues and came up with nothing. It was as if the killers had never existed.

Little did Lund and Gorski know that the killers would soon return.

The history of Clovis City, with the political intrigue and assassinations, encouraged Colonel Gorski to keep his opinions to himself. He confided in Evart, Lund and Collins and no one else. He never let Lyss know what his true thoughts were due to his lack of trust in the man. His behavior might have been mistaken by some as paranoia, but for the Colonel, his actions were due to his experiences from the dangers of the past. In his mind, his plans were designed out of pragmatism so that his sons would be safe.

CHAPTER ONE

Yuri Gorski finished his psychological evaluation and waited in the lobby of the medical section on space station Cy-7. He had been the first of the witnesses to the murder to finish the testing. Gorski was watching the Empire news broadcasts on the wall of the lobby when Lieutenant Garrison and detective Bennington approached him.

"Let's take a walk," Bennington told Gorski.

Gorski followed the two men out onto the main walkway of the space station. They walked in silence for a few moments.

Gorski finally stopped and put his balled fists on his hips. "What is this all about?"

The two men stopped and turned to see that Gorski was not amused.

"We are going to level with you kid. The murder of your friend will become huge news. You know who Drayton's father was?" Bennington asked.

"Yes, I know. He was my friend," Gorski answered as he recalled the months he spent with Love-Easter at the Spetsnaz camp and their over three years at the Academy. Other than the death of his mother, Gorski had never lost someone so close.

"Well, we are concerned with Empire Security," Bennington told Gorski. "If Pastor Love-Easter starts getting upset at how our investigation is proceeding, he might cause problems. I am sure Drayton spoke of his father and what he is capable of."

Gorski nodded, "Yes, Dray told me many tales regarding his father. What does this have to do with the investigation and catching his murderers?"

"Everything," Bennington said softly as his eyes darted around to ensure they were not being watched. "We need for you and your friends to say nothing to the media, or anyone else for that matter. Any news media involvement could have a negative impact on what we are trying to do here."

Gorski nodded, "I agree that the news media cannot be trusted. But what leads do you have? Have you been able to locate any of the six men based on our descriptions?"

"No," Bennington admitted. "It is possible they escaped the station before we quarantined and sealed the docking bay. It is also possible they are still here. I wanted to let you know we will lift the order sealing the station in an hour. But we believe you and your friends might be in danger. So we would ask that you remain here for another day or two, just in case."

Gorski frowned at this. "Michel and I have one of our major flight examinations tomorrow. We are supposed to fly over the Forbidden Region with our flight battalion. We have to get back."

Garrison put his right hand on Gorski's shoulder. "I understand your pressure from the Academy. Detective Bennington and I will inform your Dean that you are material witnesses to the murder of your friend. I have no doubt you will be allowed to retake the Forbidden Region tests. Can you work with us on this?"

Gorski wanted to cooperate with the men as he wanted Drayton's killers caught. Gorski also understood that, with the six attackers still on the loose, they could all be in danger of retaliation. Gorski looked back at the medical section entrance, "Let me talk to my friends. They won't be happy, but I can convince them to remain here for another day or two. If you think it will help solve Drayton's case."

Bennington smiled, "Thank you for understanding. And yes, this helps us immensely."

"And you will contact the Dean, let him know why we are not in class?" Gorski wanted assurances.

"I will contact the Dean personally," Garrison promised.

"I hope you don't mind if none of us want to stay at the Baroness for the next two days," Gorski told them and then thought of their other friends that were still on the space station. "Can we speak with the cadets that came here with us? I think what happened to Drayton should come from me. I don't want them all finding out from the media."

"That would be fine. Give me a list of names and we'll round them up. We'll put you, Staszko, Gillis, Evart and Papanikolaou up at the military executive suites." Bennington told Gorski. "You will be very comfortable there. We will round up your other friends and set you up in one of our executive meeting rooms."

"Thank you," Gorski told the two men.

"When you finish here at the medical station, my security guards will escort you to your temporary quarters," Garrison told him.

The two men left Gorski alone in the hallway. Gorski had the sinking feeling that they were either lying or holding something from him. Either way, Gorski remembered the lesson he learned as a child and that was trusting authority in the Sikorsky regime could get you killed. Gorski resolved to warn his friends as something was not right and they needed to find out what was really going on.

Drew Harrison woke up with a horrible hangover. The two women that shared his bed had already left, not even bothering to wake Harrison to say good bye. He took some painkillers, ordered coffee and cranberry juice from the hotel catering service and jumped in the shower. He could feel the pain killers eliminating his splitting headache as the soothing water crashed onto his body. He turned off the water, stepped out of the shower and ordered the computer to air dry him. He looked into the bathroom mirrors as he was being dried by the high powered air blowers that were hidden in the bathroom walls and noticed the two female marine security guards standing behind him. Harrison turned around to make sure his eyes were not playing tricks on him or that he was not still under the influence of tequila and whiskey. The mirror did not lie; the two uniformed guards were standing in his hotel room.

"What the hell?" Harrison demanded.

"Sorry, sir." One of the guards said. "By order of the station commander, you need to come with us."

Marco Andolini had pulled an all-nighter at the poker tables. He had his sixth cup of coffee next to his massive pile of chips at a table of nine players. The dealer was an android from the Poker Pro computer program championed by the Allen Corporation. During the course of the night, players came and went. Marco was on a roll. He received his two cards from the android dealer. King of hearts and King of diamonds. Pocket kings, great hand for Texas Hold 'Em. Marco announced he was raising the blind and put in $2,500.00 in chips. Several of the players at his table folded their hands. Only one player called the bet.

The android dealer showed the three community cards, king of spades, two of clubs and seven of hearts. Marco had hit three of a kind. He was mulling over in his mind whether to slow play his set or bet. That was when he felt the tap on his shoulder. Marco looked to see two marines standing behind him.

"I am kind of busy, here guys." Marco told them.

"Finish your hand, and come with us," one of the guards ordered. She was just under seven feet tall and was one of the hybrid humans that had her DNA altered by doctors in the Eastern Europe region of old Earth. She looked more like a bear than human and Marco correctly concluded that tangling with her would be a losing proposition. Her brown fur seemed to bristle as she waited for Marco to obey her directive.

Marco cursed to himself. He was rolling and his competition seemed to enjoy giving away their money. He bet $4,000.00 in chips and the other player quickly folded his hand. Marco collected the chips from the pot as he wondered what he did this time to warrant sending the Marines out to fetch him. Normally Marco would be interrupted by some sports fan wanting his autograph or some jealous man upset that a disloyal girlfriend had slept with him. Marco turned to the soldiers as he motioned to the floor manager that he wanted to cash out. "Can I cash in my winnings first?"

Klaus Rhinehard woke up with April Mejia in his arms. She was asleep with her head on his chest. They had spent the evening talking about their mutual love for flying space craft. He learned much about the lovely woman, why she decided to become a pilot, her family, what life was like growing up in Chile. He enjoyed hearing her describe her home town and talk about her family. He was most interested in the number of earthquakes that her family survived during her childhood. When they were both too tired to continue the conversation she had asked if she could stay the night. She extracted a promise from Rhinehard that he would not try to have sex with her. Rhinehard promised her and he kept his word even though she felt soft in his arms. He was hungry and was trying to determine whether to wake Mejia or let her sleep longer when his hotel room door flew open. Two security guards walked in.

Mejia sat up, startled by the noise of their boots.

"Klaus Rhinehard? April Mejia?"

"Yes?" Klaus sat up.

"Come with us," the guard ordered.

Each one of Gorski's friends were escorted to the military service quarters on the space station except Jack Harcourt. The security scans positively identified him departing the space station shortly after the cadets had been released from the Tank.

Those that had been rounded up were taken to a conference room to find Gorski, Gillis, Evart, Staszko and Papanikolaou waiting for them. The five looked exhausted and Mejia thought that they looked as if they had not slept at all. They greeted one another. The Andolini brothers hugged everyone in the room, as was the norm for them. Once everyone arrived, Gorski determined it was best to tell them the news right away.

"Last night, a group of six men attacked Elektra at her hotel room," Gorski began and stopped speaking out of anticipation of the emotional outburst that was imminent.

"What the hell!" Dominic Andolini angrily blurted out.

"Are you okay?" Arch Frazier went to her.

"She is okay," Gorski said over the cacophony of voices shouting questions. "She is unharmed. When the attackers entered her room, Elektra was able to get off a scream. Fortunately, Dray was across the hall and heard her. He rushed in to protect her. In the fight, the six men murdered Dray. I am sorry to tell you all like this, but he is dead."

The group began shouting more questions. Gorski heard Dirk Fenster ask about the status of the investigation. Harrison was demanding to know who did it. Harumi Shigeta had tears running down her cheeks as she hugged Dominic. Rolf Rhinehard stood silently in the corner as the others hugged and wept over the loss of their friend.

Gorski spoke over everyone, "Look, I have been speaking with the chief of space station security and the chief investigator. They are doing everything they can to locate the killers. Dray's family will be contacted soon and I am certain that the news media will be all over this story. We have been asked to give no comments to the media. The investigators are going to keep us informed as to what is happening."

"We can help them," Harrison offered.

"No," Gorski told his friend. "We need to let them do their jobs. Now, the five of us are going to remain behind for a day or two to answer questions of the investigators. The rest of you need to pack up and get back to New Edinburgh. You all have classes tomorrow."

"He was our friend," Mejia protested. "We want to help find who did this."

"I appreciate that, April." Gorski said softly. "We all want that. But for now, you need to all go about your lives at the Academy. That is what Dray would have wanted. Now, until the authorities apprehend the killers I want all of you to stick together. Do not go out alone. Travel in pairs. You will also hear some things from the news reports. Remember they never report everything. Be careful out there. You all understand me?"

They were all nodding that they did.

"There is a shuttle leaving in an hour, I want all of you on it." Gorski's mood indicated that he would not entertain any debate on that issue. "Drew, Marco, Dominic, I need a private word with the three of you."

Gorski and the group walked out onto the main hallway. All of the group had to collect their belongings from Baroness Hotel. Once they were around crowds of people, Gorski passed a stack of folded papers to Harrison.

"These are computer print outs of the attackers based on the descriptions we gave the CID," Gorski whispered to Harrison. "Something big is happening here. I can feel it. Use some of the stolen computer access identifications we have hidden in our dormitories and find out who these people are."

"I am on it," Harrison promised.

Gorski moved next to the Andolini brothers. "The hotel security did not have their scanners operating at the time Elektra was attacked. I think there might be a cover up for an inside job."

Marco and Dominic were both dumbfounded by that information.

"You mean they shut down the security?" Marco asked.

"Yes," Gorski answered. "I want you both to find out who the management is at the Baroness. Who owns and operates it. Who the security employees are. Find all of those things out. Once we have those answers, we might be able to pin down who was involved in Dray's murder."

"You can count on us," Dominic told Gorski.

"And guys, keep an eye on Elektra when she gets back to the Academy. She saw these men and she described them. She stabbed one of her attackers. I saw him, and it looked like the wounds were fatal." Gorski stopped walking. "I think they may try and finish her, either for revenge or to keep her silent. But we need to make every effort to protect her. We might want to get some of the other girls in the dorms like Kat Strahovski, Ann Harcourt and Mia Nguyen to lend us some assistance in watching her."

"Agreed," Marco said as he hugged Gorski. "See you at the campus."

Gorski watched his friends walk to the docking bay where the shuttle to New Edinburgh awaited them. Gorski was confident his friends would be careful. Now that he had seen them off, Gorski and the others had work to do while they were still here on the space station.

FORBIDDEN REGION

CHAPTER TWO

The apartments given to junior officers were quite spacious, with several bedrooms, extra closet space, extra bathrooms, large kitchens and full of comforts that were not afforded the cadets in the dormitories. Cadet Pierre Zerbe had woken up early out of habit, mainly since he was a light sleeper. He was anticipating the day more than others due to the fact his flight squadron was going to be tested by his flight instructors over the Forbidden Region in the Southern Continent. Zerbe needed to make a good impression on his teachers so that he might be considered for selection on the Tournament Team competition that would occur many months in the future. Zerbe walked around the large apartment and marveled at how well the Space Command took care of their officers. He found the kitchen was full of all of the necessary cooking machinery, including the all-important coffee maker. He verbally asked the kitchen computer to brew a pot of coffee and then sat down on the silver leather couch that was in the black carpeted dining room.

FORBIDDEN REGION

Zerbe waited for the woman in the master bedroom to wake up. He had already showered and dressed into his cadet flight suit of blue and green so that he could make it to roll call early. He met his sex partner at a local bar the previous night and she was more than willing to bring him to her apartment for a night filled with lust. She was a Lieutenant in the Space Command and worked as a transportation pilot with the Space Station Cy-7 Squadron. Zerbe smiled when he heard the compute voice notify him that the coffee was ready and he stood up on his feet, walked into the kitchen and poured himself a cup.

Reesha Bedrossian sauntered into the dining room from her master bedroom. She was wearing a red satin bathrobe and had a smile on her orange and white furry face. Her long tail was wagging this way and that as she moved close to Zerbe and kissed him on the cheek. She was a Kotek, a half human and half feline hybrid that was a breed of beings created by scientists on old Earth as a part of a program to make humans better, faster, stronger and more agile. She was slightly shorter than Zerbe and had a slender body. Her physical appearance was of an upright woman until one concentrated on her cat like eyes and ears and her body covered with soft fur. Zerbe was one of the few humans that enjoyed sex with the Kotek women and he especially liked the scratches that they would leave on his back and chest during their love making.

"Sleep well?" Zerbe asked her as he kissed her lips, feeling her whiskers tickle his cheek.

"What do you think? You are an amazing lover, Pierre Zerbe."

"Can I see you again tonight?" Zerbe asked after he sipped on some of the coffee. He smiled as he watched Reesha open her refrigeration unit, pull out a glass container of milk and begin drinking from it. The Kotek's were able to eat like normal humans, but would occasionally act like a domestic cat and want to drink cold milk. Most of the Kotek's that Zerbe had met over the years did not drink coffee or juices and were primarily meat, fish and chicken carnivores and consumers of dairy products.

"Yes, I would love to have you come over tomorrow," Reesha smiled as she placed her glass container of milk back into her refrigeration unit. "I have to fly a round trip run to the space station and should be back by four in the morning. I can change the security codes at the entrance of my apartment so you can just let yourself in. You don't mind being her alone until I make it back?"

Zerbe smiled and recalled how amazing the woman was in the bedroom, "Girl I will wait for you as long as it takes."

Ressha rubbed her forehead against Zerbe's shoulder as a domestic cat might do and meowed. Zerbe put his arm around her and could hear her purring as he ran his fingers through the fur behind her pointy ears. She licked him on his cheek with her rough tongue and smiled at him.

"I really like you, Pierre Zerbe," Reesha told him.

FORBIDDEN REGION

"I feel the same," he assured her. He began to wish he could spend the morning with her, but the Forbidden Region and his examination were waiting for him.

Admiral Jordan Seward, United Nations Space Command (retired) had received many awards over the many years of service to include selection as an Astronaut Training Specialist, Medal of Valor recipient, United Nations Meritorious Service Medal recipient and Professor of Aeronautics and Astronauts at the Clovis Academy. Before Seward could finish his first cup of coffee he received the Holo-com call from Criminal Investigation Division chief Charles Bennington with little emotion. Seward listened as the CID Chief of Space Station Cy-7 detailed the death of cadet Love-Easter and that several of the cadets that had witnessed the event were being detained for their own safety. Seward terminated the three dimensional conversation with the investigator and leaned back in his chair in his plush office at the Academy. Seward was now in his sixties and would spend his mornings reflecting on his illustrious career. Often his thoughts would concentrate on the fate of his two missing sons.

He had raised all of his children to become officers in the United Nations Space Command. Most of his children grew up and rejected the military life for other career choices. Two of his sons followed the example set by their father and became capable pilots and officers. Each of those sons had gone missing on separate missions with no clue as to their fates. In memory of his sons, Seward decided to spend his retirement teaching young astronauts the tactics of flight and warfare so he could be instrumental in keeping the young students alive. In the last few years, Seward was learning that his students were more of a danger to themselves than any enemy. The young seemed to take unnecessary risks as if they believed themselves immortal. He often speculated that his missing sons made that fatal error, thinking themselves invincible and rushed to meet death. One son disappeared on the Battle Cruiser called the Bismark which had been sent to survey a new Earth-like planet in the far reaches of space. The entire ship vanished without any evidence of her fate. His other missing son had been a member of a Fleet that vanished into an anomaly in space while pursuing an enemy alien race. The Space Command lost all communications with the Fleet years ago. Seward never gave up hope that one day the missing ships and their crews would be located.

Seward mourned the death of Cadet Drayton Love-Easter. The young man showed promise both academically and in his leadership skills. Love-Easter truly cared for the cadets under his command. Although Love-Easter had been involved in some bar fights and some other minor altercations, he never participated in hazing or harming the younger cadets. In fact, Love-Easter would actively protect the new recruits from acts of violence. He watched out for their safety and on occasion fought to keep them out of harms way, just as cadet Love-Easter had done, protecting a sophomore cadet.

FORBIDDEN REGION

Seward sent an e-mail to the Clovis Academy Dean of students and to some of the Professors alerting them of the news regarding cadet Love-Easter. He pulled out a legal pad with about thirty names scribbled on it. Seward had been working toward preparing a list of qualified seniors and one underclassman to compete in the annual Tournament of Semiramis Moon. The Tournament was a matter of great pride and standing for the Academy that won the event. Each of the four Academies would assemble a team of ten cadets to compete. The goal was to capture the other three teams to be the victor. Clovis Academy had never won. Seward believe that the thirty cadets he had been evaluating had a chance due to their intelligence, their grades, their leadership qualities and their never say die attitude.

Love-Easter was the second name on Seward's list. Seward drew a line through the young man's name. The first name was Cadet Colonel Eamon O'Grady. The third was Cadet Captain Yuri Gorski. Seward pursed his lips in deep thought. Gorski would have been the one Seward was going to recommend to the Dean to lead the mission. Seward was certain the Dean would overlook Gorski's occasional bar fights. But now that Gorski was in the midst of a murder investigation of another cadet, the Dean would not be favorable of selecting Gorski to represent Clovis Academy at the Tournament. Seward counted his twenty-nine other listed cadets. It was standard to send a minimum of five cadet pilots to the competition. Seward drew an arrow from Gorski's name to the near bottom of the list and wrote in the name of cadet Captain Amir al-Nasser in Gorski's place.

Seward was hesitant in making the change in the order of his list. He had also written in the names of cadets Drew Harrison, Marco Andolini, Lester Brey Gillis and Michel Darcel Evart. Seward knew he would have to move all of them to the bottom as well. Enough was enough. The young lads had caused enough trouble and the Dean would only want students at the Tournament that would look out for the Academy's best interests. Seward believed in his heart that Andolini, Evart and Gorski were fantastic pilot candidates, but the Dean would be against their selections.

Seward stood up and went to his coat rack and found his flight jacket. It was five o'clock a.m. At six a.m. all pilot candidates were to report for their semester flight examination. They were to fly over the planet of New Edinburgh and each cadet was to stun one of the creatures in the Forbidden Region and then return safely to base camp. It was not as easy a task as it might sound. The creatures were intelligent and in years past there had been some casualties among the cadets. Caution was the first order of business.

The Forbidden Region was the title given to the Southern Continent of New Edinburgh. The land mass was larger than Asia on old Earth. The Glorious Leader had decided to not conquer that region and allow the indigenous creatures to live as normally as they would have but for the interference by humans. All of the settlements, factories, businesses, the Academy, scientific and farming areas were located on the Northern Continent. The Western and Eastern Continents were scheduled for invasion by the military, but no dates had been given for invasion.

Although the Northern Continent had been "tamed" for the most part, there were still pockets of large flesh eating creatures roaming there. They were aggressive, seemed to always be hungry and they loved to feast on human flesh and bone. The major settlements had built large walls, similar to the water dams on ancient Earth, to keep the larger reptiles out. An occasional dim-witted civilian would stand on the walls and taunt the creatures only to learn the hard way that some of the monsters could jump many feet in the air and the taunting human would become dinner. The winged Cawlers were the biggest danger as they could fly in from above, trap their dinner in their large claws and then fly away all within seconds.

Yes, life on New Edinburgh could be dangerous.

Seward walked down forty flights of stairs to get to the air field. He preferred walking to the elevator lift as it helped keep him in shape. When the Admiral strode out of his building he put on a pair of sunglasses as he had never grown used to the red-orange glare of the sky. Although the atmosphere and oxygen content was similar to Earth, there had been no firm scientific explanation for the different color sky.

The cadet astronauts, just over eight hundred of them, would fly one-man Allen Corporation Fighter Type CC76A2 space crafts to the Forbidden Region and back. First designed in 2376 the Year of Sikorsky, the Allen Corporation Fighter Type CC76A2 space craft were lightning fast ships and capable of reaching speeds of three times the speed of sound. The Allen Corporation had updated the model and all of the CC76A2's were given to the Academy's for training purposes. The Allen family had boasted that the newest model, the CC76A3, could reach speeds of five times the speed of the A2's. The ships were all exactly forty feet long from front to rear and eighteen feet tall at their highest point. They had metallic landing gear keeping them upright on the landing field. The front of each ship was cone shaped and the rear was shaped in a rectangle. The space craft all had wings extending four and a half feet from either side. If they were going to fly into a real battle, each wing would be able to support two rockets and extra laser batteries. The canopy was covered by four feet by two feet transparent metallic glass as an observation point. The ships were powered by a hybrid nuclear and solar engine. The technology to harness both solar and nuclear energy had grown over the centuries. Most of the solar cells, when fully charged, could power the ship completely. The nuclear power was only utilized when the solar cells became too drained. The rear of each ship had four exhaust vents and counter-measures that could be used to throw off an approaching heat seeking missile.

FORBIDDEN REGION

All of the A2's were painted a bright yellow with the exception of the Cadet Captain's ships, which were white. The flight instructors flew ships that were painted black.

Admiral Seward would be joined by several other pilot instructors to grade the students. Each cadet's ship computer would record when they score a direct hit on one of the creatures in the Southern Continent. The indigenous population of New Edinburgh resembled the dinosaurs of old Earth from the Triassic or Jurassic period which led to the coining of the phrase "Dinosaur Wars" during the early settlers battles with the creatures.

The training ships were armed with stun lasers only. No rockets or laser vaporizer cells were allowed on training missions. This was to protect the life of the animals and to protect the cadet that was accidentally hit by another ship, which happened every trip.

As Seward approached the vast paved landing field, three cadets in green flight uniforms with blue flight jackets approached him. The first was Captain Amir al-Nasser. He was a twenty-two year old man from France and held out that his genealogy was from Syria. Most of the Middle East and Africa had been annihilated in two separate wars and the survivors immigrated to other nations. The first was the Oil Embargo Wars of 2140. The second conflict that had the most devastating losses on the African Continent from the old Earth was the war against the Akarzdamedians. Due to the massive loss of life in those two wars, the chances of meeting a person with an old Middle Eastern surname was rare. The Wars cost the lives of over a billion people. When the Akarzdamedians attacked, it was the first war in which humanity faced an alien invader. The cost in human life was a terrible price to be paid, but humanity came together and repelled the alien horde. In the aftermath of the war, the United Nations Security Council seized control of the Earth governing responsibility and installed Vladimir Sikorsky as the Secretary General.

Amir al-Nasser had dark skin and short dark hair. He was physically fit, a great student with a strong grade point achievement. He was married to three wives, all arranged marriages, and had two children and one of his wives was pregnant. Seward had noted that al-Nasser possessed the potential of being a good leader one day and had proven to be one of the best pilots participating in the test run.

The second was Cadet Captain Porfirio Cardenas, a twenty-three year old member of the "Peace and Reformation Movement" as taught by Pastor Love-Easter. Cardenas even had the tattoo of the cross on his right cheek to symbolize openly his acceptance of Christianity. Most of the followers of Pastor Love-Easter had the cross branded onto their faces, but this was illegal under the Code of Military Justice. Accordingly, Cardenas and other cadets had to settle for a tattoo and refuse the hot branding iron. Cardenas was the son of Rear Admiral Alejandro Cardenas, who was the commander of the Empire's Eighth Battle Cruiser

Fleet. Cardenas and his siblings were raised as so-called "military brats" due to their father choosing the space command as his career. As a child, Cardenas saw several solar systems and visited numerous planets. He learned by watching his father and other soldiers what was expected of an officer. When he was old enough to choose where he would attend college, Cardenas selected the Clovis Academy over other civilian academic options. His childhood dream was to become a pilot and the Academy promised to afford him that opportunity.

While attending the Academy, Cadet Cardenas married and had produced two children. He was five foot nine inches tall, had light brown skin and light brown eyes. Like al-Nasser, Cardenas was a good student and was respected by the young cadets in his Flight Company.

The last student pilot approaching Admiral Seward was Cadet Captain Mary Johnson Lincoln. She was the daughter of Colonel Jamal Lincoln, who served as an army commander aboard a Battle Cruiser. She had two older brothers, three older sisters and four sisters that were younger than her. The ten Lincoln siblings led lives similar to that of Cardenas as military brats. Lincoln was African-American, twenty-two years old, slender, stood about six feet tall and had long dark hair. She was striking in her looks and had many men competing for her attention. Even her baggy flight suit could not hide the curves of her body that turned men's heads as she walked by. She was the former girlfriend of Yuri Gorski. Their break up was an emotional one, from which Lincoln carried some unresolved feelings. Lincoln was considered by Seward and her peers as one of the best fighter pilots at the Academy. Her father had allowed her to learn to fly ships well before she came to the Academy, which had given her an advantage over the other cadet pilots. Lincoln was probably about a year or two advanced in her experience level over the average cadet pilot. She was well liked and respected by all due to her amiable personality.

Lincoln, Cardenas and al-Nasser saluted the Admiral. Seward returned the salute. They were the first four to arrive at the long landing strip. Seward was impressed by the three cadets as he always taught his students that the best leader was the first to arrive and the last to leave. Leadership by example goes a long way to ensure morale and loyalty among the troops.

"At ease," Seward told them. "Climatology scans indicate no chances of any Dust Storms or other potential dangerous weather conditions. A wonderful morning for an around the world flight."

"Yes sir," Al-Nasser answered. "We hope to make you proud of our progress."

Seward nodded, "I am sure you shall. I am glad the three of you are early to hear what I have to say. I have some distressing news."

"What is wrong, sir?" Lincoln asked. As she was speaking the four saw Cadet Captain Marco Andolini running toward the air field. Running behind Andolini were several other cadet pilot candidates, April Mejia, Klaus Rhinehard, Dirk Fenster, Jack Harcourt, Tina Martinson, Roy Starr, Angus McWilliams and Melissa Harcourt.

Seward sighed to show he hated being the messenger of bad news, "Cadet Drayton Love-Easter was murdered two nights ago on Space Station Cy-7."

He saw Lincoln's shocked reaction. In the years she spent with Gorski, Lincoln had become close friends with Love-Easter. Lincoln bit her lower lip as tears were forming in her eyes.

"How?" She asked. Love-Easter had been very kind to her over the few years she had known him and she could not imagine why anyone would want to harm the man.

"Love-Easter was defending a young cadet named Papanikolaou from an attacker. The investigators indicated they have caught the killer and he is in custody."

"He was defending Elektra? One man did this? Dray just came back from Spetsnaz training. He was a hand to hand combat machine." She paused and covered her eyes as the tears began to fall freely. Love-Easter had beaten down over a dozen men by himself in a bar fight that she had participated in over a year earlier. "He was too good, no way. Not possible that one man could beat Dray. No."

Cardenas was also moved by the news since he was a devout follower of the religious movement of Love-Easter's father. "Who did this? How, sir?"

"The killer stunned him and then slashed his throat," Seward responded. "Love-Easter bled out before any help could arrive."

There were now many more cadets arriving. Marco Andolini was forming the cadets into Flight platoon ranks.

"And Elektra? Is she hurt?" Lincoln inquired as to her friend.

"She is fine," Seward answered. "She is still at the station, with the others involved."

"Which were who?" Al-Nasser asked.

"Gorski, Evart, Staszko and Gillis," Seward answered. "Which means that some of the underclass students will have to lead Gorski and Evart's squadrons today."

Other flight cadets began assembling on the flight field. Seward saw Jurgen Doernitz, Rolf Rhinehard, Cara Perez Guerrero, Blossom Li, Lupita Calderon, James Cobb, Dino Black, Pierre Zerbe assembling with about another hundred cadets that Seward had not yet learned their names. More were arriving every minute. They were forming their ranks, platoons of four squads, eleven to a squad forty-four to the platoon, with a platoon leader out front, centered on their formation and exactly twenty paces from the front squad.

Cadet Captain Marco Andolini was watching the progress as Lincoln approached him. They hugged. She had tears in her eyes.

"Were you there, Marco? When it happened?" Lincoln asked, holding her friend close.

"No," Marco told her. "I did not see it happen. But we were all on the space station together. Before we returned to New Edinburgh, Yuri gave us some instructions. He thinks there might be some sort of a cover up. I have never seen Yuri so, what is the word I am looking for, secretive."

Lincoln looked up at Marco, blinking her lovely brown eyes at him. "What do you mean by that?"

Marco whispered in Lincoln's ear, "According to Yuri and Elektra, it was not a one man show. There were six attackers. The Hotel Baroness security cameras had been cut off and Elektra swore she mortally stabbed one of the six."

Lincoln whispered back in his ear, "It would seem Yuri might be right to be secretive. They announced that they caught the lone killer. He is in custody and he was not injured. If Elektra did stab the man, then he should be in the ER."

"Or the morgue," Marco finished the thought for her.

Marco was silent for a moment. He put his arm around Lincoln's shoulders and guided her away from all of the approaching cadet pilots. When they were out of what he felt was the range of the cadets listening in, he said, "Dray was cut up really bad. Elektra, Yuri, Les, Jen and Michel gave detailed descriptions of the attackers. There was an Asian man, a tall muscular dark skinned man and one with tattoos all over his body. Yuri had a conversation with the CID on Cy-7. Yuri felt that they were going to sweep what happened to Dray under the rug. He asked us to try and find matches based on the computer print outs of the attackers."

"And how did you guys get those print outs?" Lincoln asked. Then she thought better of the question. With Gorski, Gillis and Harrison involved, there was no telling what they pulled off to secure the information. "Never mind. I don't want to know."

Marco smiled at that, "Yuri wants us to look into the ownership and operation of the Baroness Hotel. He wants to know who the manager is, security chief, the workers and the whole operation. Think you can help us out?"

Lincoln nodded, "Anything for Dray."

"I knew I could count on you Mary." Marco hugged her again. "Now, listen. You know Yuri is kind of paranoid about authority."

"Because of what happened to his mother," Lincoln said in Gorski's defense.

"Yes," Marco said softly as he recalled the day he held Gorski in his arms when Melita Gorski and her platoon were blown up. "I was there, remember? He cried on my shoulder. I didn't even know his name at the time. Yuri thinks that we need to travel in pairs or even larger groups and I agree. Don't be walking around alone Mary. There is no way Dray got taken down by one man. I fought by his side too many times. Dray could take on ten men by himself."

FORBIDDEN REGION

Lincoln nodded, "Let's get back to our troops. We have a test mission to fly. When we return, we need to continue this conversation."

They began walking back to the growing formation. Marco looked at her and smiled, "I missed you this weekend Mary."

Lincoln nodded, "I have missed you to, Marco. Was he with the gypsy?"

He only nodded affirmatively to her question. He was certain that Gorski's relationship with Staszko was still painful for Lincoln. She and Gorski had parted, gone their separate ways and Gorski replaced her quickly with Jen Staszko.

Andolini and Lincoln did not notice that one of the cadets, Jurgen Doernitz was being picked on by two bullies on the other side of the airfield. Doernitz was a twenty year old orphan that had stowed away on several space ships over the years as a child. He, along with his older sister, Freya, was forced to spend a life of hiding in fear, begging or stealing for their next meal and moving from ship to ship. Although Doernitz never talked to others of his rough childhood, his sister had confided in others regarding their sad youth. According to Freya, the two had to escape from an orphan camp to avoid being sold for slave labor. They fled Sikorsky's Planet aboard a large transport ship and panhandled on space stations and other planets. But one day their luck changed for the better. They were able to sneak onto a U.N.S.C. Battle Cruiser that was commanded by Captain Yamamoto. When Jurgen and Freya were finally caught by security, Yamamoto and his wife protected the homeless children and then adopted them. The two lost children finally had a home of their own with the Yamamoto family. The Yamamoto's raised them as one of their own and fully integrated Freya and Jurgen into their large group of children. Jurgen Doernitz became interested in learning to fly ships growing up as the Captain's son. At a young age of ten, Doernitz was flying one man fighters as Captain Yamamoto's wing man. By age eleven, he was flying Raumschiff's. By age twelve, he knew how to strip and repair the engines of both space crafts. By age thirteen, he could operate the Astro-Navigation station on the Command Station of Captain Yamamoto's Battle Cruiser. Doernitz spent a lot of time in his youth with the engine technicians and engineers. By the age of sixteen he had learned everything there was to know about the repairs and operations of a Battle Cruiser engine. By age seventeen he joined his sister, Freya, as a cadet at the Clovis Academy. He was sponsored in as an entering cadet by the newly promoted Admiral Yamamoto.

Although Doernitz was one of the most talented pilots at the Academy and a master at engine building and repairs, he was not adept at hand to hand combat. The campus bullies knew this about the young man and took advantage of Doernitz and his unwillingness to fight. The only person that had defended Doernitz was the man that had married his sister Freya. That man was Cadet Captain Porfirio Cardenas. Doernitz had been cornered twice before by the abusive cadets of the infamously named Bragg Gang and Cardenas had to intervene to protect his brother-in-law. Doernitz never gave others an acceptable explanation as to why he would not defend himself. Many cadet pilots thought that the twenty year old Doernitz was a coward. Others saw him as a physically fit young man that could easily stand up to aggressors, but chose not to fight. Doernitz stood six feet tall, had broad shoulders, good muscle tone from spending time in the gymnasium and he had long blonde hair and blue eyes.

Doernitz was checking his assigned ship when fellow cadet pilots Angus McWilliams and James Cobb spotted him alone. McWilliams and Cobb were members of the dreaded Bragg Gang. Although Gorski's troop was the subject of much gossip, William Bragg's group were the outright bullies of the Academy. They would beat up young cadets for their money, steal their clothes and food. Sometimes the Bragg Gang would just assault another cadet for the pure sport of it. They were also known for conducting acts of hazing against the new cadets. All of the Bragg Gang were avoided on sight by the other cadets. Yuri Gorski and his friends had several run ins with the Bragg faction the previous year. Gorski and his team always came out on top, leaving all of the Bragg followers beaten.

McWilliams and Cobb were much bigger and stronger than Doernitz. McWilliams had developed a reputation for assaulting younger and lesser experienced cadets. Cobb was more of a follower and did whatever McWilliams told him to. They approached Doernitz as he was checking off his fuel gage and solar cell levels.

Doernitz turned and saw the two standing in front of him. He smiled at them, "Hey guys." It was not the first time that McWilliams and Cobb had decided they could push around Doernitz. The two men had started beating Doernitz once before, about three months earlier, until Porfirio Cardenas intervened on his behalf.

Cobb, with both hands, shoved Doernitz in his chest and into the side of his space craft. "You little shit! You think we are going to allow you to go on this training session and ruin the grade curve again?" Doernitz was wincing with pain from the impact against the metal frame of his assigned space craft.

McWilliams grabbed Doernitz by the front of his flight suit. "I would have gotten an A on the last flight test if you hadn't ruined the curve!" He was referring to the Around the World timing test. Doernitz had been the fastest pilot that day, flying around New Edinburgh in record time and beating the second place finisher by twelve minutes. Some of the other cadets blamed Doernitz for ruining the grading curve for that exercise.

"Come on guys, I didn't do anything," Doernitz protested. "The last mission had a lot of pilots that scored high. My scores didn't ruin any curve."

FORBIDDEN REGION

Cobb punched Doernitz in stomach, causing him to double over. He was coughing and in obvious pain as his arms wrapped around his midsection.

"Fight back you coward!" Cobb taunted Doernitz.

McWilliams slapped Doernitz with his open right hand across the cheek. Doernitz head whipped to the right from the impact. The gathering crowd heard the sound of the impact and could see a red palm print on Doernitz' cheek.

"You're a loser!" McWilliams spit in Doernitz's face. "You were tossed away like garbage by your parents. Nobody here likes you. The girls won't have anything to do with you. All you do is go fishing on the weekends and hide behind your sister's husband. Go back to the dorm rooms where you belong. You fly this mission and ruin my grade curve and I will give you an ass kicking like you have never known."

Doernitz looked down at his flight boots recalling that Admiral Yamamoto had instilled in Doernitz the ideals that violence was always a last resort. He did not want to fight and bring dishonor to the Yamamoto family name. McWilliams slapped Doernitz again. When Doernitz head was moved by the impact, he could see that there was a crowd of other cadets watching. Some of the witnesses were members of the Bragg Gang. Doernitz could see that Roy Starr, John Gauthier, Derek Regehr and Basil Varek were holding back the crowd, protecting McWilliams and Cobb from any interference.

"I'm not leaving," Doernitz looked Cobb and McWilliams in the eyes defiantly. "I am flying today and I will be an officer and a gentleman. I will be a Space Command pilot."

"Then you better fight back, man," Cobb taunted him. "Cause we are going to beat you down so bad they will have to carry you to the infirmary."

"I will not fight you," Doernitz said firmly. "Fighting solves nothing."

Cobb and McWilliams began laughing. McWilliams right arm began to cock back, his hand balled into a fist. McWilliams decided that it was time to hurt Doernitz bad enough to convince the younger cadet to leave the Academy. Before McWilliams could deliver the blow, a cotton white hand grabbed the cadet's arm. McWilliams cursed and turned to see Melissa Harcourt smiling up at him as she was holding his hand firmly in hers. Her dark hair was blowing in the New Edinburgh wind. Her milky white face was beautiful, as all of the Children of Athena were. She was smiling and blinking her eyes at McWilliams. His eyes began to soften and he slowly lowered his right arm to his side. Cobb also began to react differently, his scowl was slowly fading into an expression of serenity and his balled fists began to loosen up, his fingers opening. McWilliams looked as if he had been placed into a trance. His anger at Doernitz was turned to caring and compassion for the Harcourt woman. McWilliams was certain that Harcourt had put some form of spell on him. McWilliams and Cobb both found Melissa Harcourt irresistible and they could not move.

They were completely under her control.

Melissa Harcourt was using some of her inherited powers to cause the two men to fall under her suggestions. She was controlling their minds with ease. It had not been the first time she had used her abilities on others in such a manner. The two men seemed to be under her control quickly, either due to the two men being mentally weaker than others or that her talents had grown in power. She began sending out her body scent to soothe the other Bragg Gang members. Cobb looked over at his other friends and observed that they were also experiencing some form of personality change. Roy Starr was slowly walking away with his head down in shame. Varek, Gauthier and Regehr were already walking toward their ships. In a matter of seconds, Harcourt could read in the minds of Cobb and McWilliams that she could order them to strip naked and dance in circles if she so desired.

"Go back to the formation," Melissa Harcourt told them softly.

Cobb and McWilliams slowly backed away from her and then walked back toward the large gathering of cadets. Cobb was weeping.

Harcourt reached up to Doernitz and softly touched his face. Doernitz could feel the stinging pain from where he had been slapped fading. The onlookers could see the redness on his cheeks disappearing. April Mejia and Klaus Rhinehard were standing in the back of the crowd and were in awe of the healing abilities exhibited by Harcourt. They were both going to move in and help Doernitz just before Harcourt had beat them to it. Mejia and Klaus' intervention would have been much more violent than Harcourt's had been.

"I'm Melissa," she told him as she used her free hand to touch the other side of Doernitz face. The pain was soon gone. "You need to stand up to these guys otherwise they will never leave you alone." She moved her hands away. Doernitz was amazed that she could heal small wounds just by her touch.

"Thank you, Melissa, you are very kind. My face doesn't hurt anymore."

"One of my many abilities. Why won't you fight them? You look strong enough to take them." She asked him, while feeling the muscles on his arms.

"Fighting is not any way to solve differences."

Melissa laughed, "Then you need to find a new career field. Weakness is Provocative. Haven't they taught you that yet? All they teach us to do here is to fight and kill."

Doernitz pointed in the direction of McWilliams and Cobb, "What did you do to them?"

Melissa pointed to her snow white face, "Look at me. I am one of the Children of Athena freaks. I am able to emit a scent that makes the opposite sex find me attractive, or even irresistible. I can also make them want to follow my every command."

Doernitz looked into her face, studied her hair, her eyes and her lips. "You are not a freak. You are the most beautiful woman I have ever seen."

She laughed and began walking away from Doernitz. "It's my body scent; I think I got some on you. See you up in the skies Jurgen Doernitz."

Doernitz was speechless as he watched the Harcourt woman walk away. He saw the crowd of his fellow cadet pilots. They all looked at Doernitz with differing reactions. Some pitied him, others despised him and others just could not believe he refused to fight back. One by one, the cadets began to go back to their formation. It was close to time to move to the supply officers and check out enviro-suits and hand lasers.

Doernitz followed the small crowd to the supply building.

Each of the eight hundred cadets was required to wear a complete enviro-suit during the Forbidden Region flight examination. That edict was the same for commissioned pilots when flying the small fight ships. The Space Command had determined many decades ago that a small crack in the small space craft could lead to loss of oxygen in the cabin or expose the astronaut to the space void. Other planets and moons had different atmospheres. If an astronaut found it necessary to eject without an enviro-suit, they would be facing certain death without the suit. Thus, the standing order was to require all pilots to wear the suits, even for a simple training mission.

The cadets were also issued hand held laser pistols which was also standard issue for any flight mission. But for this specific test, the lasers were given as a precaution to any ship malfunction or accidents. If any cadet was to crash in the Southern Continent, they would find themselves surrounded by thousands of kilometers of dense, virgin forest and thousands of species that were deadly to humans. Some of the creatures were small flying blood suckers that transferred a deadly poison into the blood stream of the human victim. Others were much larger meat eaters and they were always hunting and seemed to be constantly hungry.

Many of the early human settlers died at the hands of these creatures. The marines, the army, the space command and military intelligence fought the Dinosaur Wars in the Northern Continent for years. The death toll was high. The humans that conquered the Northern Continent found that the indigenous animals of New Edinburgh were not to be toyed with. Humans had to understand their boundaries and respect the animals.

On past Forbidden Region runs, several cadet pilots had met their demise. Some of the larger reptilian creatures could leap into the air and they would swat the fast moving ships out of the sky. One of the largest creatures had a large tail that could be used as an effective weapon to strike down potential prey and space ships. Some of the large creatures had learned to throw

FORBIDDEN REGION

large objects at the crafts. And then there were the mechanical issues that might force a cadet to eject, then that cadet had to survive on the surface until rescued. No cadet that had to eject had survived the experience as they had become meals for the predators in the Forbidden Region.

The eight hundred cadets dressed in their enviro-suits quickly. They were all in their second year or higher. No first year cadets were allowed on this test. Most first year cadets were still in the virtual training stage and still learning on simulators. Some were still trying to master the anti-gravitational training. They would not be permitted to fly an actual craft until their second semester began.

The cadets lined up into formation and waited for the order to board their space crafts. They watched as the cadet Captains took roll call. The cadets noticed that Captain Gorski and Captain Evart were missing. Two of the flight instructors, Captain Hibbert and Captain Kowalski, were calling roll for those companies. Everyone else was present.

Admiral Seward marched to the front of the formation. "Cadet Blossom Li and Cadet Jack Harcourt, front and center!" The two cadets, that were serving as platoon leaders, did an about face, and then double timed it to stand before the Admiral. They saluted Seward who returned their show of respect. Seward had determined that the Forbidden Region test would be a good challenge for Li and Harcourt. They were two of the junior cadet pilots that were in line for Flight Corps Battalion Commander in the next year. Although there were other senior cadets present for the mission, Seward wanted to observe the leadership abilities of Li and Harcourt.

"Lieutenants," Seward began, "We have two commanders missing. Cadet Li, you have temporary command of Company B on this mission. Cadet Harcourt, you will take charge of Company D. Don't let me down."

"Sir! Yessir!" Jack Harcourt and Blossom Li said in unison. Seward excused them and they both ran as fast as their legs would carry them to their new temporary positions.

Jack Harcourt felt pride that he had been selected. But he was also sad that his friends, Gorski and Evart, were not present in their rightful positions. Harcourt had no idea that he had made an impression on Admiral Seward. Harcourt felt out of place, standing before his classmates, taking charge of them. He hoped he would make all the correct commands and decisions. He was nervous. He wondered if Li felt the same.

Seward barked his next set of orders, "Cadets, don your helmets, secure them and check oxygen pressure!" All of the cadets began putting on their enviro-suit helmets. The cadets all checked their left wrists where the oxygen levels were regulated. None of the cadets indicated any malfunctions with their oxygen supplies.

Mary Lincoln looked over to al-Nasser and he gave her a thumbs up to signify that he was ready for the adventure. Lincoln wondered if anything ever made al-Nasser nervous. Lincoln had made the Forbidden Region Run twice before. Lincoln knew the dangers of this test. Each time she participated in the Run she found herself apprehensive. She personally witnessed a cadet die the previous year when his ship crashed and then he was covered by the aggressive Sand Spiders.

"Board your space craft!" Seward ordered.

The cadets began moving to their ships. Lincoln felt a tap on her shoulder and turned her head to see that it was Porfirio Cardenas. "Trust in the Lord. You need to have faith." He told her.

"Thank you." Lincoln swallowed. She noted Cardenas was extremely calm. She walked to her space craft as she could hear other ships powering on.

Lincoln climbed up the side of her craft using the hand and foot holes that were crafted into the ship as part of the design. She sat in her cockpit and pulled the metal harness over her shoulders that rested in her midriff. "Computer, close observation glass."

The top of the ship slowly was enclosed by a sheet of protective transparent metal and glass. But this was not average household glass. The glass tops of all Allen fighter ships were constructed out of a special metal that was transparent. The metal had first been mistaken for diamonds when discovered in an asteroid belt. The engineers and scientists were successful in molding the metal to serve as the observation windows on all space craft. More of the precious metal was located on the planet named Cootron. Several moons also yielded the precious metal. Most flight personnel called the metal "glass" but it was given another name by the scientists, Murdockiniam, after the first geologist to discover the useful element.

Lincoln waited till her transparent canopy closed completely. Once it had, she ordered her computer to start the nuclear engine. She heard the soft hum of the engine working, which reminded her of the purr of a domestic cat. She ordered her solar cells to take over the fueling of the engine. She then spoke to her company.

"F Company, this is Captain Lincoln. Stay with your wing man. We will be flying at nine hundred kilometers an hour. Stay in tight formation. Platoon Leaders, report whether all pilots are prepared for lift off." Lincoln then waited for the reports. The squad leaders reported first and then her platoon leaders. All of Company F was ready to proceed.

Lincoln felt her adrenaline level rising. She loved to fly. "F Company, lift off!"

Lincoln told her computer to display her three dimensional manual controls. The green steering and control panel appeared before her. She placed her hands on the half-moon steering control and moved it upward which caused her space craft to slowly rise up into the red-orange sky of New Edinburgh. Her Company was following her lead. She looked down and saw that Amir al-Nasser and his company was also leaving the landing strip. She located Jack Harcourt and Blossom

Li leading the companies of Evart and Gorski. All of the ships were rising and in formation.

Dirk Fenster was comfortably flying in formation next to his wing woman. Fenster liked how the Allen fighters maneuvered with little effort expended by the pilot. Fenster's family had built another version of the one man fighter space craft, but the United Nations Security Council voted to approve the bid of the Allen Corporation instead of the Fenster's. As he was flying his small craft, Fenster recalled as a little boy how his grandfather was livid that the hated Allen Corporation had out bid him. Fenster had flown the version of the ship built by his family. He had to admit that the Allen's seemed to manufacture a better product on this line. He hoped that the test mission went by quickly as he wanted to contact his friends and check on the current status of the investigation on Space Station Cy-7. April Mejia had invited everyone to her dorm room after the Forbidden Region Run for dinner. She was going to cook up her absolutely delicious enchiladas with her amazing queso, Spanish style rice and refried beans. Mejia was beautiful, smart and a fantastic chef. If Klaus Rhinehard didn't marry that girl then he was a fool, Fenster thought to himself. It would be nice if Gorski, Evart, Staszko, Gillis and Papanikolaou could attend the dinner.

As the flight progressed away from Clovis City and in the direction of the Forbidden Region, Fenster's thoughts drifted to the events of the past weekend on Space Station Cy-7. Fenster had never experienced the loss of a friend before. He, like the rest of the underclass men and women in Gorski's Gang, was distraught over the murder of Love-Easter and the attempt on Papanikolaou. Fenster had hoped that the leaders of the group would have trusted him more with the secrecy he observed. With his family connections, Fenster was in a unique position to obtain valuable information to help Gorski and the others. Fenster hoped that the exclusion of the juniors, sophomores and freshmen was not due to a lack of faith in the minds of Gorski, Gillis and the Andolini's. One thing was for certain, Gorski had an intensity on his face that Fenster had never seen before.

Porfirio Cardenas was constantly looking over his Company, making verbal orders to some of the cadets if they were making any deviations on their flight pattern. They were in tight formation as required by their regulations. He allowed himself to relax a little. It would take about three hours to reach the Southern Continent. He hoped his performance would earn him a spot on the Tournament Team. He had applied the previous year and had not been selected. Selection on the team was a great asset to ones resume and generally would give priority later in choice of duty stations. He looked to his left and saw Jurgen Doernitz flying next to him. Not only was Doernitz his brother in law, but he was also his wing man. It gave Cardenas a feeling of serenity knowing the best pilot was flying beside him.

Amir al-Nasser had similar desires to compete in the annual Tournament. He had already asked Admiral Seward about his chances of being selected to the ten person team. Al-Nasser was a skilled pilot and a dual major, learning mechanical engineering as well. During their conversation, Seward indicated that the dual talent would give al-Nasser a better chance of selection than a cadet that only studied one area of knowledge. Al-Nasser needed to make his family proud by not just being on that team, but bringing the winning trophy to Clovis Academy for the first time. His three wives and two children were depending on him.

Angus McWilliams asked his computer to connect him ship to ship with his friend James Cobb. "Hey, Jimmy! I am going to tag me one of those Verburgt!"

"You know those are against the rules of the mission, man." Cobb replied. "We are supposed to stick with the smaller creatures."

"The smaller creatures?" McWilliams sneered. "Those are for wimps. I am going to take down a big dinosaur today."

Cobb was silent for a moment, thinking he was glad he was not McWilliams wing man. "Dude, have you told Tina what you are planning to do?"

"Tina Martinson is my wing man, or should I say wing woman only because al-Nasser assigned her with me." McWilliams said. "I do not give a damn what she thinks."

Cobb had no response to that. He concluded that his friend McWilliams was just a little out of control.

CHAPTER THREE

Yuri Gorski and Jen Staszko were finished with their complimentary breakfast from the military mess hall on Space Station Cy-7. The food was fairly bland. Gorski found that the air recycling units needed new filtration systems as the oxygen on the space station had a foul stench. He had never noticed the smell during his previous trips to the station. He wondered if the extended stay on the station caused him to become more aware of the shortcomings of life on such a facility.

Gorski and Staszko were sipping on coffee and eating pastries when Les Gillis sat down at their table. The mess hall was large with about seventy eight foot long tables that could seat eight soldiers to each. There were several marines, technicians, pilots, military intelligence and army personnel enjoying their daily breakfast. Gorski was paranoid enough regarding Dray's murder that he was counting the number of soldiers at each table, their unit designations and their ranks. Gorski had noted that there were five Military Intelligence enlisted women at a far table dining on eggs and bacon. Their solid black uniforms were neatly pressed and form fitting. The highest ranking woman at the far table was a Sergeant First Class. There were five female and two male seven enlisted Marines at a table to the north of the hall, each with the rank of Private and dressed in their Class C camouflage fatigues. They had laser pistols attached to their hips and two of the women had laser rifles slung over their shoulders.

No one else was at the table occupied by Gorski and Staszko until Gillis sat next to them.

Gorski noticed that Gillis had a perplexed look on his face. "Spill it Les. What is it?"

"I was doing research on the virtual computer base." Gillis said. "They had a news release posted. They claim they caught Dray's killer."

"Killer?" Staszko repeated with a suspicious tone to her voice.

"Yes, killer. Singular. Not plural." Gillis stressed. "And it was man named Alexi Khartov. The news bulletin claims he confessed to killing Dray and that he acted alone."

Gorski was tapping his fingers on the table looking at the table of the five Military Intelligence women, wondering if they were spying on them. "I knew that they were going to try and sweep this under the rug." He sipped his coffee and thought for a moment. "Khartov, why does that name sound familiar?"

Gillis looked down at the table as if embarrassed. "Because the night of the attack, I had slept with this guy's wife.

Remember the girl I introduced you to at Tinkerbelle's? Alejandra? That was his wife."

Staszko chuckled, "Ah, Les, you have the worst luck with women. Does anyone know that you played hide the salami with his wife that night?"

"No, at least the news is not reporting it. The news also reported that Alejandra is missing. Yuri, you were right as always. There is a major cover up brewing here."

Gorski continued drinking his coffee as his eyes kept roving around the room watching the service men and women like a hawk. "We need to get Elektra and Michel. We deserve to take in some shopping at some of the stores today. I always liked the women's clothing stores." He smiled at Staszko. "I want to buy you something nice to wear."

Stasko frowned at her lover. "Yuri, how can you think of shopping at a time like this?"

Gorski put his hand on hers. "Because at the privately owned mall stores, no one will record what we say my love."

Gillis stood up, "Right. I'll go get the others." He walked out of the cafeteria, first picking up an apple on the buffet line and began eating it.

Lieutenant Garrison had been summoned to the security section of the Baroness Hotel. He had been escorted by a young lady wearing the hotel uniform to the waiting area in Ella Ragnarsson's office. Garrison was given a cup of coffee and left alone. Garrison waited for about ten minutes before Ella

Ragnarsson came from behind another door and smiled at him. She was wearing a skin tight white top and black mini-skirt with high heeled black shoes. Garrison thought her outfit was a little too revealing for an office atmosphere.

"I am sorry to have kept you, Lieutenant." Ragnarsson approached Garrison and shook his hand. "Please. Come back to my office."

Garrison followed the woman to the back security area. He saw several Baroness Hotel employees working at computer stations, monitoring the front of the establishment. Others were watching the floors and the back receiving area. Ragnarsson led him to her private office. Garrison walked in behind Ragnarsson and saw a thirty by forty square foot office, with nice dark blue carpeting and light blue walls. She had a painting that depicted a violin next to a burning candle on the left wall. The right wall had a thirty-six by forty-five inch painting of a snow covered mountain with an etched cherry wood frame. Her desk was also made of cherry wood and had a small computer sitting on the top. She had two black leather chairs for guests and motioned for Garrison to sit in one of them. On the back wall behind Ragnarsson's desk were two college degrees that had her name in bold print.

Ella Ragnarsson had been directed by her employer, Alfred Rosenburg, to get close to Garrison and earn the trust of the space station security chief. Rosenburg had made this request of Ella in the past, with other men in other situations. She was experienced in the art of seducing men, able to gain their allegiance and even manipulate them to do her bidding. She had done extensive research on Garrison. He had been engaged to be married before he was commissioned into the service. His fiancé died in an electrical storm on planet Cootron. Those storms could be predicted by climatologists within hours of the event. Unfortunately, Garrison's betrothed could not get to the safety of the buildings in Cootron in time. She and several other engineer technicians were fried to death on the planet surface. Ever since that tragic event, Garrison had been alone.

As Garrison settled into the chair he watched Ragnarsson sit in hers. She smiled at him. "Thank you for taking the time to visit with me."

"You are welcome." Garrison said. He wondered what the meeting was all about.

"I know you are a busy man, Lieutenant." Ragnarsson began. "So, I will get right to the point. My manager and I are impressed with how you handled the murder investigation regarding Love-Easter. We are also grateful at how you maintained the confidentiality of the entire episode. Had word gotten out about these men somehow getting in to our hotel and attacking guests, well, it would have caused our reservations to dip dramatically. Our financial bottom line would have suffered."

She stood and paraded her shapely body as she walked to her door and closed it. She came back and gently brushed her right hand over Garrison's left shoulder. She sat down on her desk, facing Garrison. Her mini-skirt was exposing her shapely legs to him. She was clearly up to something, Garrison believed.

"In addition to being in charge of this locations' security, I also have the responsibility of recruiting new management and security personnel." Ragnarsson was studying Garrison's face for any reaction. She could tell that the officer was checking out her body. It was in his eyes. "We have a new location that we have finished construction for on planet New Edinburgh. We have two on Cootron and one on the Martian Colonies. I need to fill four open security chief positions in the next month. The pay is quadruple your current salary."

Garrison drank from his coffee cup. "Are you asking me to apply for one of the positions? To leave the service?"

Ragnarsson nodded. "You have been in the military intelligence ranks for nine, going on ten years? You have gone from the rank of Ensign, to Lieutenant Junior Grade and now you are a full Lieutenant and in charge of a space station security. The only way for you to make Lieutenant Commander is to obtain a transfer to a Battle Cruiser. And we both know that those positions are extremely competitive."

"How do you know so much about that?" Garrison asked.

Ragnarsson was twirling her hair with her left index finger, "Because I read, I study and I am well connected in certain circles. We need capable employees like you. That is why we are willing to pay so well. And if you decide to accept the offer, you will be trained here by me for the next month." She stood and walked over to him. She stretched her legs out and slowly sat in Garrison's lap. She leaned forward and whispered in his ear. "You and I could enjoy some fringe benefits together. Mmmmmm?"

Garrison allowed her to pull his arms around her waist. She was kissing his ear. He found her irresistible and began kissing her on her lips. She was undressing him as his hands were exploring her body. Before he knew it he was making love to her on her desk and then they were on her floor. Garrison knew he was being manipulated, but it was the most amazing job of manipulation he ever had the pleasure of experiencing.

Gorski and Staszko met Gillis, Evart and Papanikolaou in the main hall of the space station. There were military service individuals walking this way and that, civilians and other employees. Gorski observed a small group of civilians with orange hair and light blue outfits walk by. The orange hair was a dead giveaway that they were obviously tourists from the settlements from either Cootron or Athena. Gorski motioned for his friends to follow him to the escalator located to the left. The five cadets rode the moving steps up three levels to the Mall level. There they found many large and small stores for clothing, foods, wine, liquor, high tech electronics, dental offices and other random types of establishments.

As they walked together Gorski began talking so only his friends could hear him. "You all know the news? They pinned Dray's murder on one guy."

"We know." Evart answered. "Elektra and I saw his picture on the government news broadcast. He was not one of the attackers."

"And the Dray's family already issued a statement accepting the findings." Gillis added, thinking that there was a conspiracy similar to the assassination of heads of state from ancient Earth history. The real perpetrators were never apprehended in those past cases. There was almost always a person wrongfully accused so that the real culprits could go undetected. "So as far as the murder investigation goes, it is case closed. They got their confession and the real killers go free."

Gorski led them to the entrance of a fancy clothing store. "We all have to be cautious here. We are surrounded by enemies. Since we are the only ones that know of Dray's true fate we are five loose ends to whoever did this."

"What are you suggesting?" Gillis asked.

Gorski continued to lead the group around the store. "We need to leave the space station immediately. They kept us here under the cover story that the news media would not be able to interview us. I think they kept us here to buy time to figure out what they want to do with us."

Papanikolaou had her arms crossed. She was visibly scared. "They're going to kill us."

Evart put an arm around Papanikolaou to comfort her.

"Not if we can get out of here." Gorski told them. "You see, here, we are on their turf. At the Academy, they would be on ours. We have enough friends down on New Edinburgh that would make a cover up of our deaths nearly impossible. So we need to get off of this space station tonight."

"How?" Evart asked.

"Private transport." Gorski answered quickly. "The shuttles cost nothing. But we could pay a privately owned ship to take us home. If we stay on Cy-7, they will come for us tonight. We might be able to defend ourselves somewhat. But if we end up in the Tank or some other less than neutral location, then we would certainly be done for."

Gillis stopped in front of the group and watched a squad of Army Weapons enlisted men and women march past them. Gillis waited until the squad was out of hearing range. "I know that we have used private transports before. Dirk uses one all the time and tells me the owner of the ship is completely reliable. If we can get word to Dirk, he could arrange a no questions asked trip back to the planet surface. We leave and tell Garrison nothing. They will figure it out soon enough that we skipped out. But by then we would be long gone."

"Right." Gorski smiled. Gillis was always on the same page with Gorski. "Michel, you remember that virtual computer store owner you met here about a year ago?"

Evart frowned at that. The individual that Gorski was referring to was a person that Evart had hoped to forget about. "What do you want me to ask him to do?"

"Get a message to Fenster, one that cannot be traced to us here on the station." Gorski said. "Get him to get us a transport, see if he can make the arrangements for us from New Edinburgh. The less computer chatter by us, the better."

Evart nodded. "I am on it. Can I take Elektra with me? She knows computers better than I do."

Gorski smiled at the younger girl. "Yes. It is better that we stay in pairs. Be careful you two. The station is filled with MI enlisted men and women. We need to assume that they are not our friends at this point."

"Got it, we trust nobody but ourselves." Evart indicated his agreement with Gorski.

As Evart and Papanikolaou walked away, Gillis noticed that Penelope Smith (Rosenburg) had walked into the store. She was searching the business attire clothing racks. She was wearing a black business jacket and a skin tight long skirt. Her stiletto heels accentuated her shapely legs. Gillis motioned with his head to Gorski and Staszko.

"Did she follow us?" Staszko wanted to know.

"I don't think so." Gorski tried not to look directly at the woman.

Gillis shrugged, "I think I will just go ask her straight up if she is stalking me."

Gorski smiled at the suggestion. Gillis was focusing on obtaining information regarding Drayton. "Very good idea, Les. Jen and I will hang back and keep an eye on you."

Gillis walked over to where Penelope Smith (Rosenburg) was shopping. He found a black, backless and low cut cocktail dress on one of the display racks. Gillis picked the dress off the rack and approached her.

"I found this and I thought how nice it would look on you." Gillis told her.

Penelope seemed genuinely startled. Gillis deduced from her reaction that she had not been following them at all. By the look in her eyes, he concluded that she did not remember him. He held the dress up for her to see.

"And who are you?" Penelope more demanded than asked. She was angry at herself that she could not recall the name of the young man before her. In her business, knowledge was power. And lack of knowledge could be fatal.

Gillis held out his hand to her, seeing the anger in her eyes. "I am so sorry. I thought you would have remembered me. I am Les Gillis. I was in your hotel the other night. Remember we met on the fifth floor when that attack occurred." She shook Gillis' hand and remembered him at that point. The last time she saw Gillis he was distraught over the death of his friend. "Yes, you have a very good memory, Les Gillis. I was only present for a few minutes. Again, I am very sorry for the loss of your friend."

"It was more than enough time to make an impression on me ma'am." Gillis again showed her the dress. "What do you think? You and me, meet for dinner tonight? You seem like a nice person. I would really like to get to know you."

Penelope looked the man over. Gillis felt as if she was sizing him up for a fight. Her mind was racing as she considered her response. This could not possibly be a random chance meeting. This man had to be stalking her. Was Gillis on to her brother, Caine? Was he suspicious of her? She knew that there was no possible way he would be able to learn that she was related to Caine and Darryl. Her identity as Penelope Smith was too well guarded. She decided it was in her best interests to meet Gillis and find out what he does know and what he does not. "Very well. You are much younger than what I would normally date. But, since you were bold enough to approach me, I will give you some time tonight."

"Seven at night? Massimo's? Gillis asked.

"I love Italian." Penelope said. "I will be there at seven. And, as for the dress, I already have one just like it. I will wear it for you tonight."

"I look forward to seeing you." Gillis said as he slowly backed away from her. Gillis did not think that the woman would accept his invitation. "Til tonight, then?"

She smiled at him and watched him walk away. Penelope knew that there was something more in the mind of Gillis than just getting to know her. She was far too intelligent and well educated to fall for that. She would meet Gillis, have dinner with him and determine what he was after. She hoped for Gillis' sake that he was not onto the true nature of the Rosenburg family. If she felt the need to, she would have to consider having him eliminated. Penelope cursed under her breath. She hoped that her father would punish her half-brother, Caine, for setting this nightmare in motion. She made a mental note to herself, that if the opportunity ever presented itself, she would defy her father and kill Caine herself. Caine was far too sadistic and narcissistic to be trusted.

Evart and Papanikolaou approached a business on the second level of the space station mall. Evart stopped her before they entered.

"Elektra, you are going to see some things inside this place that might be a little disturbing." He told her. "The man we are going to meet is named Sven Jorgenssen. He and I, we hooked up about a year ago. It was a one night stand, nothing serious. But, we have kept in touch since then. He was more clean cut when I first met him, so please do not hold his current appearance against me."

Papanikolaou crossed her arms. "In the last three days I have been in a bar fight, arrested and released. I was nearly raped and killed. I stabbed a man. I watched one of my best friends murdered right before my eyes. I was knocked out by a stun blast from a laser. And you think there might be some things left in this galaxy that would disturb me?"

"I know." Evart said softly. He had grown to consider her as a little sister and felt that he needed to watch over her. "I still feel protective of you. Look, Sven is one of those rogue fellows that operates a legitimate business. But, he also is involved in other ventures. When we go inside, that will be apparent to you. He is probably the biggest illegal drug dealer on this space station. So, be calm. If you react in a negative manner you might startle some of the customers. We do not want any trouble in there."

"I will be fine." She assured Evart, scowling at him defiantly.

Evart and Papanikolaou entered an internet café called "Sven's". There were several long haired teenagers, with tattoos, body piercing and brands on their bodies standing behind the bar making latte's and espresso's for customers. The customers were also covered with brands and tattoos. Many of the tattoos and brands were death skulls or demons.

Another customer had a pants zipper that had been surgically implanted in his left cheek. He was unzipping it and sticking his pierced tongue out at one of the employees.

The hair color of each customer and employee was dyed giving off a rainbow effect of multi-colors. The culture of dying hair in such a manner had started on Cootron and spread to Athena. Other planets now had many younger people copying the hair styles.

There were several rows of new age three dimensional computers in booths with wooden doors to ensure ones privacy. Papanikolaou quickly determined that the business was not very professional. The location smelled of stale body odor. There was trash everywhere. Empty plastic cups for coffee thrown here and there. Most of the customers renting the computer booths seemed to be loners and drifters. The main hall was not well lighted. The floors were metal and dull. No paintings were on the metallic walls to liven up the customer experience. Papanikolaou saw three badly dressed men at the coffee bar exchanging Empire Dollars for a package of Red Dust. Another man with long dark hair and clothes with holes in them due to being worn far too many times was checking Papanikolaou out.

She leaned against Evart and whispered to him. "Michel, why do so many civilians do these things to their bodies?"

Evart leaned down and had his lips next to her ear. "Tattoo's are pretty common as you get further away from Earth. Some of the outer solar systems you will find that many people brand themselves. Others intentionally have their arms or legs or both severed so that they can replace them with the newest metallic limbs. In my home town in France, this was not how the civilians acted."

"Nor in Greece." Papanikolaou whispered. "There were occasional tattoos or some minor body piercing, but this is just off the charts. Is it because they are so far from home?"

"Could be like a fish out of water thing." Evart responded. "Remember that the majority of the population of humanity has never stepped foot on old planet Earth. You and I are in the minority. Most of what you see here is from the styles of planets Cootron and Athena."

A man clapped his hands with joy and ran to Evart. He was one of the long haired men selling coffee drinks. He was wearing a psychedelic colored sleeveless shirt, shorts and flip flops. His deep purple hair was in braids. He had the sign of the Ankh branded on his left shoulder. On his right shoulder was another brand of the Star of David. The man had tattoos which covered his neck and lower arms. He hugged Evart.

"How is business Sven?" Evart asked his friend.

"I am blessed with lots of customers. Everyone wants to keep in touch." Sven said waving his arms around, pointing at all of the people in his business.

Evart introduced Papanikolaou to Sven. He hugged her. Papanikolaou wrinkled her nose as she smelled his offensive body odor. She estimated that this man named Sven had not bathed in several days.

"So, what brings you here my friend?" Sven asked.

"I need for you to get a message to a friend," Evart told him. "Do you have any encrypted computers with non-traceable identification numbers?"

Sven was stroking his chin, looking back and forth between Evart and Papanikolaou. He motioned with his head to follow him to the back. Sven led them down the long hall of booths. One of the customers was passed out on the floor and the three had to step over him. Sven took them into a door with large letters stating "Employees Only." He turned on some lights and led them to an old style lap top computer.

"This is an old twenty second century computer set up," Sven told them. He pressed some buttons on the device and pulled out a keyboard. "You have to type out your messages on this old device. No three dimensional technology was around when this was used. But since it is an antique, there is no tracing messages sent from this computer. The U.N. security only scans for the broadcasts from computers using current technology. For security, the Military Intelligence, or as we call them the Militzia, are pretty stupid. You type in the universal address of the person you are contacting up here and write your message. When you are done, press the "Send" button. Any questions?"

"And you are absolutely certain no one or any entity can track it?" Evart asked.

"Positive," Sven assured them. "I will give you two some privacy. I will get you both some espressos and come back in a little bit."

Sven left and closed the door behind him. Papanikoalou sat at the computer desk and began typing a message to Arch Frazier's e-mail address.

"Why Frazier?" Evart asked her.

"Because Dirk is on the cadet pilot training examination. Arch is in labs and lectures today. He checks his messages two or three times a day. When Dirk gets back, Arch can give him the instructions."

Evart smiled at the younger cadet in admiration of her ability to assess the mission and come up with a plan. "Good thinking."

Papanikolaou finished typing the message to Frazier and hit the "Send" button on the keyboard. She stood up from the chair. "I hope this works."

"It will." Evart's voice was confident. The surety in Evart's tone reassured the younger Papanikolaou. "Let's go."

"What about Sven and our coffee?" Papanikolaou wanted to know.

"That's where we are going, to get our free coffee." Evart opened the door for her. "Try to avoid the drug dealers. They are nothing but trouble."

"You don't say?" Papanikolaou said as she walked back into the dark, smelly hallway.

Gillis found Gorski and Staszko at the men's section. He walked toward them with his hands in his pockets, a large smile on his face.

"Well?" Staszko was curious.

"I think we need to find me a nice outfit," Gillis said. "I have a rendezvous with a very hot woman tonight."

Gorski and Staszko laughed and hugged Gillis.

Staszko looked at Gillis, "Forty-two Regular jacket? Sixteen and a half neck, thirty-three inch sleeves? Thirty-two inch waist and thirty-four inch length pant?"

Gillis was stunned. That was what his measurements. "How did you know?"

Gorski laughed and shook his head, "Her family used to sew their own clothes. She could size up anyone. Come on; let's get you a decent suit so you can make a good impression on Penelope Smith." The three of them began shopping in earnest.

"So, what kinds of questions would you like me to ask Penelope Smith?" Gillis asked.

"I have a long list." Gorski said.

CHAPTER FOUR

The cadet formation of Allen small fighter space craft flew across the ocean separating the North and South Continents. The ocean was a mixture of deep blues, dark greens and peppered with ice bergs that seemed to be prominent in the southern portion of the planet. The forests of the southern continent were colored for an artist's eyes, with trees that had large leaves that were colored with shades of greens red, yellow, orange, blue and white. The sand and dirt on the surface was mostly a deep purple, but there were lighter shades of purple on the beaches and in some of the areas where the dense forests were located. Some of the foliage was so thick that the sunlight could barely penetrate through it. In the horizon, the cadets could see an occasional Cawler flying high and watching their ships. The flying creature would watch them as if gauging their speed and flight pattern before dropping back down into the protection of the large tree lines below.

Admiral Seward and his flight instructors were satisfied that there had been no incidents of mechanical failure. Seward was hopeful that this flight run would end without any emergencies. In the distance there was land in sight. The main part of the mission was about to begin.

Seward and his instructors would grade on the size of the creature the cadet stuns and the number of shots taken to hit the target. Thus far, each of the cadets had earned passing grades as they maintained formation at a speed of nine hundred kilometers an hour.

Seward knew it was time to get the cadets heads in line. "Computer, patch me in to all ships." The computer indicated he was connected to the ships. "This is Admiral Seward. Captain Lincoln, take your Company in first. The rest wait until all of Company F has completed their run. Captain Lincoln, when all of your flight have scored, move to higher orbit and wait until everyone has completed the mission. Then we all fly back together. Any questions?"

Cadet Captain Mary Lincoln knew that this was her moment to shine. "F Company, follow my lead. Stay with your wing man. As soon as you stun one of the creatures, your on board computer will record the hit. You are to leave the area, reach holding pattern of twenty kilometers above at the coordinates I am sending to you. Good luck. Begin your attack patterns now."

Klaus Rhinehard asked his computer to patch him in person to person with April Mejia. "Be careful, liebchen."

Mejia laughed at the sound of his voice. "You be careful fly boy. I have to get back to the dormitory to cook everyone dinner." She smiled to herself as Rhinehard had never used any terms of endearment with her before. She found she liked it. Captain Ruiz of the Colorado had advised Mejia to find herself a serious man. Rhinehard certainly would fit that description.

"Then let's get this over with." Rhinehard said as he increased the speed on his fighter to keep pace with their flight team. Mejia was flying by his right wing. He looked over at her and could have sworn she winked at him.

Lincoln told her on board computer to switch her flight panel to manual. Her three dimensional display appeared before her. She had heat sensors to her left, which indicated a huge pack of animals to target. On her right were her weapons schematics, solar power and laser cell levels, at the top center was an enhanced view of the forest below.

Lincoln asked her computer to identify the large cluster of animals on the body heat scan. The computer replied that the creatures were Dozal's. The Dozal were flesh eaters. There were millions of them on New Edinburgh. They were hairy, most of them white but other color tones had been spotted over the years. The Dozal were all generally four and a half feet tall and their length was about five feet long, excluding their cat-like tail. The Dozal had razor sharp fangs and claws on their four paws. They walked on four legs and could run as fast as a cheetah on old earth. They were the ultimate predator, fast, silent, and quite deadly. The Dozal were named after their first known human victim, Marine Corps Lance Corporal Dozal. His body had been shredded in seconds. The poor lad never saw them coming for him. The Dozal creatures had killed and eaten hundreds of marines, soldiers and civilians during the Dinosaur Wars.

Lincoln led her flight team in the direction of the cluster of Dozal. She skillfully flew her fighter ship into the thick trees and vegetation. Lincoln ordered her flight team to negotiate rapid turns and spins to avoid colliding with the trees. The maneuvers had been learned through extensive training by the cadets in the simulators and then during actual flight tests. Lincoln closed in on the cluster of about three hundred Dozal before her. She fired and hit one in her first shot. The creature fell, stunned. The other Dozal were making a strange hissing noises. Their fur was puffing up as a defensive mechanism. The Dozal were baring their deadly fangs as Lincoln's other ships swooped down through the dense, virgin forest and began firing. The Dozal were falling as the stun lasers hit their targets. The ones that were not stunned ran for the safety of the trees. Lincoln saw one Dozal pushing two baby Dozal's into the thicker forest to protect them. Lincoln watched Mejia guide her space craft close to the ground and fire one laser burst and hit a Dozal. After Mejia scored a hit on her target, she flew her ship straight up into the sky, spinning wing over wing.

Rhinehard kept his ship close to Mejia's. He followed behind her as she made her run. Rhinehard also was able to hit one of the Dozal with a stun blast. He flew over the unconscious animal he had just fired upon. He felt guilty about firing on the creature, even though the laser was not deadly it packed a high voltage sting. He followed Mejia back up into the sky.

In just a few seconds, Lincoln's entire flight team had scored hits. Their mission was over. She flew her fighter up to the rendezvous point to wait for the other five companies to complete their assignment.

Admiral Seward was impressed that the flight squadron of cadets was composed enough to finish the assignment off so quickly. He was aware that Cadet Lincoln had spent several evenings, after classes, to work with her younger cadets on this specific mission. Clearly, Lincoln's extra effort had paid off. Seward made a mental note to award Cadet Lincoln with ten extra credit points for this training examination.

Seward ordered in E Company under the command of Cadet Captain Porfirio Cardenas. Cardenas made similar orders to his flight squadron as Lincoln had to hers. The cadets followed Cardenas into the thick forest.

Cardenas, using his screens, detected large bodies to the right of his flight. They were a pack of larger reptilian creatures. Cardenas knew that it was the dreaded Verburgt. They had been named after an Army Captain named Verburgt as he was the first to discover them. They were generally no less than forty-five feet high. Their scales were green and yellow in color. Some had different colors. Their eyes were dark, like those of a great white shark. They possessed sharp teeth and were known to eat men and women in just a few bites. Some human victims were swallowed whole. The Verburgt were known for their elongated tongues, long spiked tails, muscled hind legs, front arms that could move fast and stretch.

Since the Verburgt were so deadly and had been known to withstand stun blasts from lasers, they were illegal to approach on training exercises. The major danger was that the Verburgt had knocked ships out of the sky with their powerful tails. Every cadet was warned to avoid the Verburgt at all costs, unless they were armed with laser batteries that can vaporize a target.

Recognizing the heightened danger of the Verburgt versus the Dozal, Porfirio Cardenas made the following order to his flight group: "This is Cadet Captain Cardenas. Avoid the cluster of Verburgt to the right. I have spotted a pack of Dozal at ten o'clock. You are ordered to follow my lead to that area."

The cadets followed Cardenas without question. Jurgen Doernitz flew close to Cardenas. Flying next to Doernitz was Cara Perez Guerrero. The young woman from Mexico City stayed close to Doernitz right wing. The cadets moved skillfully into position and began to stun the fleeing packs of Dozal. Every cadet in Cardenas' flight scored hits and moved up to join Lincoln's flight above. Doernitz had been the first to hit his target and the first to rendezvous with the F Company cadets.

Admiral Seward observed as Marco Andolini led his team into the fray and was just as successful as Lincoln and Cardenas. Andolini had Dirk Fenster and Rolf Rhinehard on his flight. The two young men handled their assignment competently.

"What a rush!" Rolf yelled as he flew up into the sky with Fenster following him.

Andolini remained in the forest area until the last pilot in his flight finished the mission. Once the cadet pilot finished and flew up away from the forest, Andolini followed.

Cadets Blossom Li and Jack Harcourt also led in their flight teams and did well.

The only difference was that Blossom Li had several of her cadets stun a pack of Tree Spiders that they spotted on their flight into the dense jungle. The Tree Spiders were three feet long, had six legs, brown and black in color, and venomous. One bite from the fangs of a Tree Spider would render a human in unbearable pain for several minutes, causing convulsions, vomiting of blood and then finally death. The Tree Spiders would hide in the tops of the highest trees and wait for their prey to wander below them. They would glide down on strong strands of webbing onto the unfortunate beings, bite them, and wait for the victim to succumb to their venom. And then, they would feast on their carcass. They were similar to their cousin arachnids called the Sand Spiders, except that the Sand Spiders hid underground and waited to feel the steps of the hunted. The Sand Spiders would spring from under the dirt and latch onto the unsuspecting prey and strike.

FORBIDDEN REGION

Melissa Harcourt and James Cobb had been in Blossom Li's flight unit. Harcourt stunned two of the Tree Spiders that had been huddled together on a large, seventy foot tall tree. As she flew her ship under the tree after she scored her hit, one of the spiders fell onto her cockpit view window. She instinctively screamed until the spider slid off of her ship. She then began laughing at herself for being scared of the unconscious spider.

"That was groovy, man!" Cobb was laughing at Harcourt's expense.

Melissa turned off her communication system before cursing Cobb under her breath. "Over seven thousand cadet pilots and I get stuck with you as my wing man."

The last flight was that of Cadet Captain Amir al-Nasser. Admiral Seward gave him the order to lead his flight into the jungle.

Al-Nasser smiled. This was his opportunity to separate himself from the rest of his fellow cadet commanders. Al-Nasser had heard Cardenas, Andolini, Harcourt and Li order their flights to avoid the Verburgt. Al-Nasser knew they were forbidden to engage the Verburgt, but that directive did not mean they could not fly around the large creatures to attack a large pack of Poggies in the distance. The Poggies were fat, pink, four to five foot long creatures that walked on all four legs. Their legs were short. The Poggies were vegetarian creatures and were part of the food chain of the other predators in the Forbidden regions. The early settlers wanted to call them pigs, as they were similar to that earth animal. In fact, the farmers and other settlers to New Edinburgh raised and bred Poggies for their meat. The bacon from a Poggie tasted similar to that of a pig on Earth.

Al-Nasser was determined to demonstrate to Admiral Seward, once and for all, that he was the superior cadet Captain.

"This is Captain al-Nasser. All of A Company, stay tight with your wing man. We are moving in for our run." Al-Nasser informed them. He led the flight of cadets down into the dense forest. He looked to his right to ensure that his wing man was keeping up with him.

"A Company," al-Nasser began, "We are going to earn ourselves some extra credit points today. To the right at three o'clock is a cluster of Verburgt. We will approach them at high speed and then veer left to the large group of Poggies. When the Poggies are in view, open fire."

"Sir, are you sure about that?" Cadet Tina Martinson asked nervously. She had never questioned her flight leader before. But his current command made her nervous. She had seen the videos of how fast the Verburgt were.

"Hell yes he is sure!" McWilliams yelled. "Let's go hunting some giant dinosaurs!" McWilliams, using his manual controls, pushed his space craft into full speed in the direction of the cluster of Verburgt giant creatures. He had always wanted to travel outside the protective walls of the city to find and kill one of the many giant dinosaur species on New Edinburgh. His hope was to send the skin and skeleton back to his family in Scotland.

He thought the sharp fangs from the creatures would be a fine, original gift to send home to his sisters. They could turn the fangs into several necklaces.

Admiral Seward, viewing the events from above, became concerned immediately. "Cadet Captain al-Nasser, recall your flight. Some of your flight team might not be prepared to confront the Verburgt. Recall your flight team."

"But we are not trying to take down a Verburgt." al-Nasser protested.

"I gave you a direct order, cadet!" Seward was raising his voice, which was something he rarely did. Seward could see on his three dimensional display that McWilliams and Martinson were flying directly at the Verburgt. "A Company, you are ordered to disengage and rendezvous with the rest of the mission team."

Over half of the cadets from A Company adhered to Admiral Seward's demands. They aborted their mission and flew out of the jungle. Many others, not understanding why the order had been given, began to fly out of the forest. McWilliams did not listen. He was determined to down a Verburgt. McWilliams wing woman, Tina Martinson, was following him, but growing more and more apprehensive as each second went by. Martinson was terrified of the giant dinosaur type monsters. She kept thinking of the films she had watched of them eating soldiers from the historical videos chronicling the Dinosaur Wars.

"Angus, I am not allowed to leave you!" Martinson yelled at him. "Please, let's pull back and join the others."

By now, al-Nasser realized that the two cadets had ignored Seward's order. "Cadet McWilliams! You are ordered to back off! Disengage!" Al-Nasser was yelling at the cadet, mostly because al-Nasser felt his desire to make a big impression on Seward might have caused this. He turned his ship around to pursue McWilliams and Martinson. He could hear Seward yelling for him to come back, but he would not leave McWilliams or Martinson in harms way alone.

Seward groaned. Three idiot cadets. It happened every year. "Listen up, I am going in with two of the training pilots. Cardenas, you are in charge. Keep everyone up here, above the forest. No one else is to follow us in!"

Cardenas, Lincoln and Andolini felt they should go in, but held back and obeyed Seward. They watched as Seward guided his ship down into the forest. He was followed by Hibbert and Kowalski, two of the flight instructors. McWilliams was yelling like a cowboy at a rodeo. He had flown his CC76A2 fighter ship to about ten feet off the ground flying at about one hundred sixty kilometers an hour. He could see the forty-five foot tall creatures in the distance. McWilliams counted seven of them. Tina Martinson had matched his elevation and speed. She was flying next to him as was her duty. Amir al-Nasser was far behind them, yelling orders for them to break off their attack run. "Please, Angus," Martinson pleaded. "Let's go back."

McWilliams shook his head. "You go back. I am almost in target range of those beasts. I'm taking one down!"

McWilliams began firing his stun blasts at the midriff and lower legs of the Verburgt in the distance. He and Martinson could feel their screams of anger and annoyance. The Verburgt did not fall down as would be expected. The stun blasts only angered the giant predators.

The giants were now looking at McWilliams and Martinson's ships. The creatures were making loud rumbling sounds, showing their deadly sharp fangs. To McWilliams dismay, the Verburgt did not run away, but began to charge at his ship. And with the dense forest around him, McWilliams knew he had little room to maneuver.

"Ah, shit!" McWilliams yelled. "Pull out!"

McWilliams began to turn his ship, but he quickly realized the forest had grown denser. His only option, as well as Martinson's, was to fly right at the monsters. If they were lucky enough, they could fly around the giants and rejoin the others.

The seven creatures were still charging the two oncoming ships.

"Fire at them!" They heard al-Nasser ordering them from their rear. "If you hit them with enough stun blasts, they will go down!"

McWilliams began firing his lasers at the Verburgt. After several blasts, one of the forty-five foot tall giants fell to the earth with a resounding thud.

Martinson did not have to be told twice by al-Nasser to open fire, especially after she saw one of the monsters fall to the earth. She began firing her laser batteries wildly. Many of her blasts hit targets, others did not. Martinson was shaking with fear. She had perspiration on her forehead and upper lip. Her hands were also shaking. Martinson knew that her nerves were gone. She tried pulling her ship upward, panicking. Her ship's wings struck some of the branches of the massive trees of the forest. Martinson's right wing broke off causing a small burst of flame on the side of her ship and sending her spinning out of control. The broken wing piece twisted in the air as it descended downward until it smashed on the planet surface. Martinson was screaming in fear as she saw that her ship was going to slam into the earth. She covered her face and braced herself for the inevitable impact. Her ship hit the ground, front first, and was sent flipping end over end. Metal pieces flew from her ship in every direction; purple sand was flying in the air. Martinson could hear McWilliams and al-Nasser calling out her name, begging for her to respond to them, even over the loud cacophony of the impact and tearing metal. She screamed, hoping that her small ship would hold together enough to protect her from the monsters so the others could rescue her.

McWilliams kept firing at the Verburgt as he watched Martinson's ship crash on the planet surface. McWilliams was angry at Martinson for being stupid enough to follow him in. He had told her to go back and she did not listen. Now, he had to waste his time trying to protect her and even try the impossible, rescue her. Martinson's ship was in bad shape. The wings were torn off. The cockpit was shattered, leaving the young woman exposed. The back of the ship had dents and scrapes while the front of the ship was crushed in about a foot. McWilliams could see Martinson moving through the black and grey smoke billowing from her craft.

"McWilliams!" Al-Nasser was yelling to get his attention. "Orbit above Martinson's ship! Fire on the Verburgt, keep them away from her! I am going to try and lower my tow cable and lift her ship out of the forest."

McWilliams grunted and followed the order. He began firing at the other six Verburgt as Al-Nasser was lowering the four inch thick magnetic cable down to Martinson's mangled ship.

"Tina, can you hear me?" Al-Nasser called out on his communication device.

"Yes," Martinson replied. "I am not hurt. I feel dizzy. Can you help me?"

"I am lowering my tow cable down to your ship." Al-Nasser told her. "Stay in the ship. I am going to try and connect to your ship and fly you up above the forest. Just hang on."

"Hurry, please." Martinson was crying from fear. The simulator training had components to prepare cadets for a crash landing. But all the instruction and simulation in the Academy could not prepare a cadet for the actual event. Martinson was shaken up. She had hit her head several times during the impact of her ship smashing into the ground.

McWilliams kept firing but the Verburgt were too strong and too many. The creatures began using their long spiked tails and began swinging at the two ships. McWilliams had to move his craft up and down to avoid the slashing tails.

Al-Nasser was focused on attaching his cable to Tina Martinson's wrecked ship. He felt the impact on the side of his ship, sending his craft spinning out of control. One of the tails of the Verburgt had made contact with his space craft. Al-Nasser worked his controls to guide his craft back to a level orbit over Martinson's ship. He heard McWilliams screaming for him to get away from Martinson's ship. Al-Nasser looked up from his controls just in time to see another one of the large tails arching down at him.

All of the cadets above heard Al-Nasser's death cry. The tail slammed into his cockpit, shattering the protective glass and metal above him. His ship slammed hard to the surface. He shook his head and ran his hands over his body, to see if he had been cut in the crash. He felt no wounds but his enviro-suit helmet had been shattered. He was stunned, if anything at all. Al-Nasser sent out a distress signal to the others, letting them know that he had crashed onto the surface. Al-Nasser concluded that his ship was inoperable when he looked over his control panel. Most of the instruments were smashed from the impact of the Verburgt tail. He observed pieces of metal, plastic and glass scattered all over his cockpit. The front of his ship had crashed into the surface and was covered by light purple sand. He unstrapped his safety belts and drew his hand laser. He saw three of the Verburgt charging at him. He fired his laser several times, hitting the large creatures. The laser blasts would cause the giant creatures to stop for a few seconds and then they would recover from the electrical shock.

But the Verburgt were undaunted. When the initial numbness from the laser stun wore off, they would continue their charge toward the human on the surface. Al-Nasser tried to crawl out of his cockpit and his plan had been to use the body of his vessel as cover. As he tried to jump to the ground, one of the creatures swung its' long tail and connected with al-Nasser in his chest. The force of the impact sent him rolling on the ground until he hit a tree trunk with force significant enough to knock his breath out and break two of his ribs. His enviro-suit was torn open at his chest area and ripped over his left shoulder by the sharp spikes of the Verburgt tail. Al-Nasser knew that was bad news. Now the predators could smell his body.

Al-Nasser began crawling, trying to catch his breath, when he felt his left leg being crushed. He screamed. The pain was immense. He felt himself being lifted by his left leg into the air. A Verburgt had his left leg in its mouth. The fangs had penetrated the protective enviro-suit and torn through his flesh. Al-Nasser knew his skin had been ripped open by the fangs of the large monster. He could feel the warmth of his own blood oozing out.

Amir al-Nasser cried out in terror as the Verburgt opened its' large mouth and his tongue wrapped around the cadet Captain. He screamed and begged as the tongue pulled him into the Verburgt's mouth.

Al-Nasser was screaming: "Not like this!" He was one of the brightest students at the Academy. He had three wives that relied on him and two children. He knew nothing could save him. But he struggled in vain. He did not want to die like this, a simple meal for a giant monster. The jaws came crushing down. Amir al-Nasser felt his mid-section, just above his stomach, being torn from the rest of his body. Both of his legs were ripped to several pieces by the sharp fangs. He felt his bones in his back being crushed. Al-Nasser was spitting blood onto his enviro-suit as the second crushing chew of the Verburgt jaws crushed his chest and skull.

His communication device inside his enviro-suit had been functioning until the end. All of the cadet pilots heard the horrible screams of Amir al-Nasser and the sound of his bones being pulverized by the powerful jaws of the Verburgt.

Seward, Hibbert and Kowalski were almost at the location where Martinson's ship was. "Hang in there cadets!" Seward had heard al-Nasser's cries as he was being hunted and then eaten alive. Seward felt angry and sick to his stomach at the same time. Al-Nasser did not deserve to die in such a gruesome manner.

Angus McWilliams kept firing his laser blasts at the Verburgt. He watched the entire murder of al-Nasser on his view screen. He finally decided that it was to hell with Tina Martinson and save himself. "Sorry, girl. You are on your own."

McWilliams gunned his ship and began flying up to the sky. He could hear Martinson begging for him to come back. He ignored her pleas and kept flying upwards. She was dead anyway, he told himself. McWilliams thought, why stay and die with her? Martinson was stunned that her wing man broke the number one rule at flight school. Never leave your wing man. McWilliams had abandoned her to die. McWilliams heard and saw what had happened to al-Nasser, and he had no desire to be the next to die like that.

Seward and his two trainers arrived on the scene and began giving Martinson cover fire. They were keeping the Verburgt at bay, but there were over a dozen more approaching. They could see the smashed craft on the ground that al-Nasser had piloted. Seward counted the number of creatures on his body heat scanners. It was only a matter of time before Martinson would suffer al-Nasser's fate. Seward knew it was impossible for the three ships to protect the girl on the surface. She was as good as dead.

The creatures were closing in, screaming at the thought of human flesh and revenge for the unprovoked attack. Seward urged his men on against the odds. Then a miracle happened. Five of the cadets had disobeyed Seward's orders and had flown in from the right flank of the Verburgt. They began firing at the pack of giant creatures.

"Who is disobeying my orders?" Seward demanded.

"Sir, we could not leave our fellow cadets to die." Porfirio Cardenas responded. "Jurgen, wrap your cable around the trees like you told us you could and create the perimeter around Martinson."

"Yes sir." Jurgen Doernitz responded. When Seward had left the cadets in orbit, Doernitz had explained to the others that Admiral Yamamoto had taught him how to use the tow cable as a temporary barrier to large predators. Doernitz had learned how to wrap the cable around a sturdy object, such as a large tree, and then fly in circles around other similar items to hold the cable and create a barrier. The larger creatures would be stopped in their tracks, as the cable would block their movement from the circular area protected by the cable barrier. Porfirio Cardenas then told Doernitz that it was their duty to help. Mary Lincoln, Marco Andolini and Jack Harcourt volunteered to assist. They left Pierre Zerbe and Blossom Li in charge as the five cadets sped off to try and make the plan Doernitz relayed to them a reality.

Doernitz flew at a left angle and shot his magnetic cable at one of the trees near Martinson's ship. The cable wrapped around the tree and Doernitz flew in a fifty foot circle around

Martinson's location many times as his cable would allow and wrapped around several trees. The result was the thick cable created a fifty foot radius around Martinson's crashed ship. The cable barrier created by Doernitz went from six feet off the ground to as high as forty feet up. The Verburgt would not be able to break in. Seward and his pilots were in awe at the action of the young pilot. Seward knew he would never have thought of such a daring move. Doernitz had to dodge two large Verburgt tails being swung at him as he negotiated the difficult maneuver.

As Doernitz was attempting to make the difficult cuts to wrap his cable around the trees, Jack Harcourt used his powers as a Child of Athena on one of the largest Verburgt. He concentrated, his brow furrowed and his teeth grinding with effort, so that he could take control of the mind of the behemoth. Due to the way his body strength would drain each time he used his mind control gifts, Harcourt was painfully aware he would get only one chance to alter some of the creatures from their deadly rampage toward Martinson's location. He leaned forward in his seat as the largest Verburgt turned on one of the other monsters and attacked. The smaller Verburgt let out a cry of pain when the large jaws of the other clamped down on its neck. The smaller creature reacted to defend itself from the large aggressor. The two Verburgt were quickly locked into a life and death battle against one another. Due to the strength limitations of his powers, Harcourt released the larger creature from his control and took in several deep breaths. He would not be able to repeat the feat out of fear that his body strength would drain to the point of him passing out and crashing his ship. He was already perspiring and breathing heavily due to the exertion caused by using his mental abilities.

Even though he had ceased his mental control of the creature, Harcourt was elated to see that it was no longer a part of the pursuit of Martinson. The large Verburgt was growling as it was knocked to the ground by the smaller opponent. The trees around the flesh eaters shook from the impact of the giant monster landing on its side. Purple sand was flying into the air from the impact. Harcourt had done his job. He eliminated the largest of the Verburgt from the crisis. He wished that Melissa Harcourt had not used her powers earlier on Cobb and McWilliams as she could have helped them manipulate more of the Verburgt as he had.

Seward and his teachers kept firing as Andolini landed his ship next to Martinson's mangled craft. Cardenas, Lincoln, Doernitz and Jack Harcourt kept firing on the creatures. Andolini ordered his cockpit open as his ship touched the ground. He began unstrapping his safety harness as his friends covered him from above. He hoped the cable barrier would keep the Verburgt at bay long enough for him to pull Martinson to safety.

Occasionally, one of the large Verburgt would sustain enough stun blasts that they would collapse to the ground. Andolini jumped out of his craft and ran to the location where Martinson had crashed. He had pulled out his machete from behind his seat in his cockpit. He was breathing heavily as he reached the girl. He climbed to the top of her ship and opened her view window on the cockpit, which swung open easily. Andolini felt relieved that at least that part of the rescue came easy. He quickly looked over Martinson. She had passed out from either fear or head injury or a combination of the two.

"Marco!" It was Lincoln's voice. "My heat sensors detect about a dozen tree spiders above you. They are dropping in for an attack!"

Andolini instinctively pulled his hand laser from his utility belt. He looked up to see several Tree Spiders rapidly descending on yellow webs. The spiders had been waiting for Andolini to be exposed. The Italian took aim and began firing, stunning several spiders. Marco wished his brother Dominic was there, as Marco was not as skilled at marksmanship as his twin was. One spider landed on the shattered hull of Martinson's ship. Andolini swung his machete down on the spider before it could leap at him. Andolini cut the spider in half, spilling yellow blood onto the hull of the crashed space craft. He kept firing until he was satisfied there were no more Tree Spiders descending to do him or Martinson harm.

Andolini grabbed Martinson in his right arm, holding his machete in his left hand, just in case. He threw her over his shoulder and carried her to his ship. As he was running, a giant earth worm rose out of the ground in front of him, blocking his path to the ship. Andolini cursed. The worms could feel the impact of human footsteps. They had been known to wrap themselves around human victims, crush them and then drag them under the dirt, presumably to be eaten. Andolini held his machete steady and he waited for the worm to make the first move.

The worm was about twenty feet long and three feet thick. It had two tentacles to sense its' surroundings. There was a large mouth with a darting black tongue that was dripping black saliva. The skin color was a dark pink. Andolini noted that the worm was slimy as it slithered toward him. Andolini could hear the Verburgt screaming as they tried to breach Doernitz's cable barrier. Only a matter of time before they broke through, Andolini thought to himself. He could hear the giant dinosaurs crashing into the trees and the cable. Time was not on his side.

The tongue of the giant worm darted out at the Italian cadet. Andolini moved to his right and slashed at the tongue with his machete. The worm made a guttural noise as Andolini's blade severed the tongue. The worm started to slither backwards. Andolini ran to the side of the creature and began stabbing it mercilessly. A brownish liquid began flowing from the gashes in the worm's flesh. The worm was trying to move away from the human. Andolini decided to let the large opponent escape as he saw several Dozal charging the scene. The Dozal were hissing and growling as they ran. Doernitz cable would not stop the Dozal, they were much smaller than the Verburgt and would be able to either crawl under the cables or jump through the spaces between them. Andolini lifted Martinson into his space craft and he crawled in beside her. Andolini ordered his cockpit to close shut as the Dozal stormed his location. They began scratching the side of his space craft, growling. One Dozal leaped onto the front of Andolini's ship. It looked through Andolini's cockpit glass, growling and showing off his razor sharp fangs, red saliva dripping from its' jaws.

Andolini, using his controls, flew his ship safely up into the sky. His heart was pounding, like he had never experienced before. The Dozal that had jumped on his ship slid off as he began ascending. "I got her! Everyone break off!"

Seward and his trainers followed Cardenas, Lincoln, Doernitz, Harcourt and Andolini to the safety of the skies. They left behind several fighting mad Verburgt growling at them.

"Amir?" Lincoln asked, knowing the answer.

"He didn't make it." Seward answered. "You five disobeyed a direct order."

"My fault, sir." Andolini lied. "I talked them into this." It had actually been Porfirio Cardenas that had come up with the idea to sneak attack the flank of the attacking creatures.

"Sir, it was really my idea." Cardenas corrected Andolini. He would not allow the Italian take the blame for his decisions. "We could not leave you all there alone."

"Return to campus." Seward ordered. "You five are suspended for twenty-four hours."

As they flew their ships, Andolini ordered his computer to fly on autopilot. He removed Martinson's enviro-suit helmet. She was breathing with difficulty. Andolini pulled out his first aid kit and injected the sleeping woman with a shot of adrenaline, ginseng and some steroids to improve her strength. She was going to require medical attention.

"Admiral," Andolini contacted Seward. "I think Martinson suffered head trauma. I request permission to fly full speed back to base for medical attention."

"Permission granted to fly at Mach six." Seward replied. "Doernitz, go with him. Get Cadet Martinson back to base."

Andolini ordered his ship to fly at top speed. Doernitz followed him, elated that his plan worked and that the girl had been rescued.

Seward watched the two young men fly off at the highest speed that the Allen ships could muster. The retired Admiral flew in silence, considering the words he would use to console Amir al-Nasser's three widows. There was also the issue of Angus McWilliams. The cadet had to be punished. His actions caused this tragedy.

Seward decided that McWilliams had to be made an example of. He had to maintain order within the ranks of the cadets. Those that put others at risk by disobeying orders had no business being an officer or an astronaut. When they landed, McWilliams would be kicked out of the Academy.

CHAPTER FIVE

Penelope Rosenburg walked rapidly toward her office. Several of the Baroness Hotel employees attempted to speak with her as she was moving through the hallways in the back restricted area. Penelope waved them off. She had no patience for the mundane, daily Hotel operational questions the workers normally asked. She entered her office and instructed her computer to seal her doors. She was furious at her half-brother Caine and her family. The events that could follow due to Caine's sadistic tendencies might prove to be catastrophic for the family. Fortunately the family was able to find a person to blame the murder on. Unfortunately, the victim named Love-Easter had friends, loyal friends, which were proving they would not give up on locating the real culprits.

She sat down in her comfortable seat behind her expensive desk. She knew that Lester Brey Gillis did not want to go out with her because he was attracted to her. Gillis was going to attempt to fish for information regarding the investigation into his friend's death. Since everything occurred at the Baroness Hotel, Penelope Smith as the manager was one of the most likely persons to interview or interrogate. Gillis was smart, that was certain.

Penelope sighed. She would dress herself up, put on a show and see if this Gillis was susceptible to her female charms. Ever since all of her "corrective surgery," as her father referred to it, had been completed no man could resist the demands of Penelope Rosenburg.

"Computer," Penelope spoke, breaking the silence in her office. "Download Ella Ragnarsson's digital file on Lester Brey Gillis."

"Completed." The computer voice responded.

"Tell me, what does this man like." Penelope requested.

"Like? I do not understand the question." The computer replied.

"Tell me about his girlfriends." She clarified.

"Lester Gillis has had four relationships that Security Chief Ragnarsson could discover. The first relationship was when Gillis was sixteen years old was with Maeve O'Conner. She was one year younger than Gillis and she lives on old Earth. Their relationship ended when Gillis left Earth to attend Clovis Academy on planet New Edinburgh. Gillis next dated Ann Harcourt, a student at the Academy. The relationship was never very serious according to the investigation. Gillis next was involved briefly with a woman named Reynita Calderon. She is also a student at the Academy. The last woman that Ragnarsson could confirm that Gillis had been involved with was a woman named Sophia DuBravac, also a student at Clovis Academy."

"Broadcast digital imaging of the women please." She directed the computer.

The life size displays of the four women appeared in three dimensional form. O'Conner's visible impression was that of an attractive red headed young Irish girl with sparkling green eyes. Ann Harcourt was one of the Children of Athena, with dark hair with cotton white skin and a curvaceous body. Penelope wondered why a Harcourt would not be able to keep a man such as Gillis. After all, the Harcourt's had many special abilities to cause another person to fall in love with them. Perhaps Ann Harcourt did not consider Gillis as a long term option for her future, she speculated.

Reynita Calderon was a dark haired Latin woman, with a pretty smile and brown eyes. According to her dossier, Calderon came from a very large family of middle class stature. Her sibling group consisted of mostly brothers. Calderon was a double major in weapons and military intelligence. Her grades were decent, putting her about the ten percentile of her graduating class.

The last, Sophia DuBravac, looked eerily similar to Penelope Rosenburg. She studied the three dimensional image of the DuBravac woman.

"Damn," Rosenburg said to herself as she inspected DuBravac's image. "We could be sisters. Computer, details on DuBravac. Where is she from?"

The computer responded by informing her that DuBravac was from the Bordeaux area of France. She was fluent in five languages, held good grades, was on the cadet chess team and was studying engineering, sciences and military intelligence.

She was proficient in boxing and martial arts. Penelope thanked the computer.

She stood up and began pacing. So, Gillis would find me attractive based on my physical appearance, she thought to herself. But he also likes intellectual and athletic women. She determined the way to get to Gillis was to stimulate the young man with knowledge. The sexual part would be easy enough. But if Gillis believed he was going to be able to spy on Penelope, she was going to turn the tables on him. Penelope spoke nine languages and had three collegiate degrees, including a doctorate. Most women could not equal or compete against her.

"Les Gillis," she said under her breath. "You have met your match."

Arch Frazier returned to the dormitory room that he shared with Dirk Fenster. Frazier set his materials and back pack down on his desk. The men's dormitory rooms at Clovis Academy all had two king size beds, two large closets, book shelves built into the walls and a large bathroom with a shower, two sinks and bath tub. Across from the beds was a small kitchen area with a table, small stove and refrigeration unit. There were two desks for studying.

In the far corner next to the windows sat Dirk Fenster's pet timber wolf. She was named Theodora. She was solid black and had been a baby when Fenster bought her back on Earth. When Fenster had been accepted into the Academy, he made arrangements to bring Theodora with him. She was large and looked menacing, unless she was used to being around a person. She walked over to Frazier and rubbed against him as he pet her.

"Good girl." Frazier told her. He saw her food bowl was empty. Frazier took some bags of cut meats from the refrigeration unit. He took the food bowl from the floor as Theodora sat on all fours, watching him. She knew it was feeding time and Frazier was always more generous with the food portions than Fenster was. She licked her chops, anticipating her meal. Frazier filled her bowl with the cuts of meat from the refrigerator and sat the bowl down in front of her. She began eating it as if it were her last meal. As she ate, Frazier filled her water bowl.

Frazier went to the sink and brushed his teeth. When he finished he moved back into the bedroom. He called out to the central Academy Computer system. "Please display all new e-mails." Frazier directed. Seventeen e-mails popped up. Several were from family, two were assignments from Professors. But one said "With Love." Frazier reached out to the three dimensional display of his new e-mails and touched that one. The message opened up before his eyes. It was from Elektra Papanikolaou. That fact alone brought a smile to Frazier's face. He read her plea to assist in obtaining a private transport off of Cy-7. Frazier typed in a response on the three dimensional keyboard before him. All he wrote was: "Message received. All will be taken care of." Frazier swiped with his right hand and the message display closed.

FORBIDDEN REGION

The explorations and geology student knew exactly what to do. He and Fenster had used some reliable ships in the past. Frazier reached under Fenster's pillow for some paper money and pulled out $1,500.00 in Empire Dollars. Frazier pet Theodora one last time before he left his dorm room and walked briskly to the light rail train that would take him to the private landing strips where the self-employed pilots waited for business.

Frazier arrived at the landing strip after an hour on the light rail train and viewed approximately forty or so private transport ships waiting for business. Frazier observed hundreds of privately owned space ships that were resting on the paved landing strip. There was much activity, as was normal.

Frazier noticed that there were seven Military Intelligence Raumschiff space craft being boarded on the northern end of the strip. Frazier knew they were from the Military Intelligence branch due to the solid black color on each of them with a light red "MI" painted on the sides. The soldiers that were boarding the ships were wearing the solid black uniforms. All of the soldiers were female which could mean only one thing that these were members of the brigade of General Leta Tan. Frazier froze in place as he realized who these soldiers were. They were the enforcers of the laws of the Glorious Leader. They had a reputation for killing wantonly and leaving dead bodies behind as a warning to others. They were ruthless and showed no mercy.

Barking out orders to the soldiers was an officer that any citizen of New Edinburgh would recognize, General Leta Tan. Frazier had never seen Tan in person before. She was much shorter than he had always imagined her. Frazier recalled that Tan had ordered a crowd of protestors in Lynott's Land executed several months ago. The news broadcasts that Frazier read of the incident indicated that Tan ignored pleas from lawyer Sean Collins to allow the accused as he referred to them and the condemned as Tan called them, a fair trial before any punishment. Tan told Collins to go to Hell and had the protestors eliminated by laser rifle fire.

Frazier tried to act like he did not recognize Tan. He was terrified that he would attract her attention in a negative way. Frazier could hear a handful of civilians pleading with Tan to set them free. Frazier saw out of the corner of his eyes that there were five civilians on their knees and plastic restraints bound their wrists. Tan pulled out his laser pistol and fired at the closest of the five prisoners, cutting the unfortunate man in half with a sustained laser blast. The other four stopped talking after seeing their comrade cut down. The remaining four prisoners were young women. Frazier heard Tan order her troops to take the women on board one of the Raumschiff's and take them to Lynott's Land for processing.

Frazier had no desire to find out who the prisoners were and what they had done. He walked at a normal pace to find any of the private space ships that he had used in the past. He hoped that Tan and her MI soldiers would not pay any attention to him.

There were a few ships that Fenster always recommended and Frazier sought them out. Frazier walked up and down the landing strip until he found one. It was a cargo ship that had been a Raumschiff, about three hundred ninety feet long and forty feet high. She was painted metallic red. In white paint were the words "Blues City." That was the winner. Frazier stepped aboard *Blues City* and was met immediately by her owner, Giles Lancer.

Lancer was a man with broad shoulders, chest and gut. He had long curly dirty blonde hair, an eye patch over his left eye and a large scar down the left side of his face. Lancer had told Fenster and Frazier once that he got the scar escaping a hungry Dozal. Lancer was wearing a one piece orange technician suit that was probably fifteen years old. Lancer had served in the Space Command as a pilot and as an engineer technician. Lancer saved his pay, gambled on cards and by the time he retired at the age of fifty, Lancer had enough money to purchase the ship and he named it *Blues City*. In the background, Frazier could hear music playing by Elvis Presley, Lancer's favorite musician of all time.

Lancer smiled when he saw Frazier. He recalled that Frazier and the other Gorski Gang members were fantastic customers and they always paid in cash. "Well, hello there my man!" His voice was loud and boisterous. "What brings you here today?"

"I need to hire you." Frazier said as Lancer shook his hand. "Trip to Cy-7 and back. I need to pick up some friends there."

"Round trip?" Lancer was thinking. "Any layover time?"

"Maybe an hour at the most." Frazier told him as he looked over his shoulder back in the direction of the black Raumschiff's of General Tan.

Lancer noticed the direction that Frazier was looking. "That is the price you pay, kid."

"The price for what?" Frazier shuddered.

"The price for speaking out against the Glorious Leader. Those people were protesting over some mineral rights taxes that had just been levied."

"And so they are going to be killed for that?" Frazier was incredulous.

"Kid, you speak out against the policies of the Glorious Leader and then you die." Lancer told him. "General Tan will leave a few bodies behind as a message to others. Death is the price you pay when you exercise free speech. She will take the women back to her military base for indoctrination."

"What kind of indoctrination?"

"Tan believes that men are incapable of love. She only has women in her brigade of MI soldiers. She surrounds herself with only women and uses them to pleasure herself with."

"So she is a lesbian?" Frazier asked.

"Yes, but she is vicious and cruel. She actually hates men. In my travels to several planets and moons I have met many men that love men and women that love women. Every interaction I have had with folks that preferred or had chosen another lifestyle was a positive thing for me. They are no different than you or your friends. All they want is to live their lives in peace and find love. Just like us." Lancer paused and pointed in the direction of the black MI Raumschiff's. "They were not like Tan. She is not to be messed with, kid. Don't compare Tan to anyone. She is walking evil."

Frazier crossed his arms and looked up at Lancer. "I think I would like to get going. How much is this trip going to cost?"

Lancer picked up a spiral pad of yellow paper and began scribbling on it with his pen. "Looks like I'll need about $1,200.00 for the trip. Cash of course."

"Naturally." Frazier pulled out the cash and began counting it. He handed over the money to Lancer.

"When do we leave?" Lancer asked, counting the money.

"Right now." Frazier told the pilot.

"Just you? No cargo, no Honey Bunny?" Lancer asked. Frazier knew that "Honey Bunny" was Lancer's code for a girl. The *Blues City* had several compartments where privacy for romance could be achieved, and with view ports to see outer space. Fenster and Frazier had taken advantage of the romantic rooms on Lancer's ship. The rooms were always clean and well stocked with wine and champagne. Lancer always told them that he believed in excellent customer service. Lancer's attention to the customers' needs was why Fenster and Frazier always came back.

"We will be bringing some people back with us." Frazier told him.

"Very well." Lancer said as he started flipping switches on the control desk. "It's your money my friend. Strap in. We will be in space in about two hours."

"Great." Frazier smiled as he sat down in the co-pilot seat. He was glad he could help his friends in need and was looking forward to seeing Elektra again.

Lieutenant Garrison walked into his office at the Security Station on Space Station Cy-7. He observed several criminal investigators working on cases. Garrison closed his door to his office. He sighed heavily. He was aware that Ella Ragnarsson only had sex with him to insure his cooperation in the cover up of the Love-Easter murder. Garrison looked over his wall with his Degree from the Academy, his large printed announcement of his commission into the U.N.S.C. He recalled how proud he was the day he repeated his oaths. One was to seek out justice and protect the innocent. The framing of the Khartov man was just wrong. Garrison felt dirty that he had played any role in the recent events.

Garrison decided that he would do something about it.

"Computer," Garrison called out. "Download to a disk all facts gathered in the Love-Easter murder investigation. Include all of the DNA evidence and each and every witness statement. Download the descriptions of the perpetrators."

The computer silently did as instructed. A small round disk dropped from the computer panel on Garrison's back wall. Garrison picked up the diskette and placed it in a hard plastic cover. He placed the disk in his top left breast jacket pocket. He intended to give the disk to Gorski and his friends. But, in case the young lads from Clovis Academy were killed on the way back to New Edinburgh, Garrison made another copy. He instructed his computer to send as an E-Mail Document, or EDOC for short, attachment all of the information to the only flag officer Garrison trusted, Admiral Cardenas.

Garrison stood up and straightened out his uniform. He knew his office was being monitored. By tomorrow, he would either be dead or re-assigned. Garrison walked quickly out to the main lobby of the Security Headquarters. He found a young marine security guard standing at attention. He told the service man to find Yuri Gorski's current location. He instructed the young man to contact him as soon as Gorski was found.

Garrison left and rushed down to the Docking Bay. He observed hundreds of people, soldiers and civilians alike, arriving and departing the space station. Garrison boarded the next Transport back to New Edinburgh. He walked calmly to the pilot section and showed his security clearance badge to the young female pilot.

"Type in to your computer that the following five civilians boarded this transport," Garrison ordered her. "Yuri Gorski, Michel Evart, Les Gillis, Jen Staszko and Elektra Papanikolaou." Garrison watched the pilot do as he had instructed. "This is a matter of Universal Security. You never saw me."

"Yes sir," the pilot said as Garrison departed.

Garrison moved quickly out of the Docking Bay area. He had a sense that he was being followed. Garrison felt his Holo-com device buzzing. He answered the call. It was his marine at security headquarters. They had located Yuri Gorski in the mall area, shopping for clothing. Garrison thanked the marine and walked as fast as he could to give the information he had to Gorski.

Ella Ragnarsson was filing her fingernails when her computer alerted her that Garrison had made a copy of the Love-Easter files. Ragnarsson threw her nail file down in anger. It was time to take action. She had warned the Rosenburg family that Garrison should have been eliminated. But, the directive came to bribe the man. Give Garrison the job offer, was what Alfred

Rosenburg demanded. Ragnarsson warned that the job offer would not work. She had been right.

Magdalena Rosenburg also had her spies out on the universal computer system. Although Magdalena was now a wife and mother, she still maintained her ties as a hired killer. Magdalena had once wiped out an entire village for the Rosenburg's. The villagers at the settlement owed big money to the Rosenburg family. The Rosenburg's hired Magdalena and her band of mercenaries to make the dead-beat villagers an example for others. They accepted the job as the pay was exceptional. They were to kill everyone, leave no survivors. Approximately four hundred men, women and children died in that attack. Magdalena had personally killed over thirty by her own hand.

When Alfred Rosenburg made the marriage offer, Magdalena readily accepted. Her mercenary team continued to take assassination missions over the years as she managed them from a distance. Magdalena called upon her former co-workers from time to time to protect her family. When Magdalena learned of Caine's blunder on Space Station Cy-7, she contacted her mercenary team to be ready to strike at a moments notice.

Magdalena heard her computer beeping in her private office at the Rosenburg Ranch. She had programmed her computer to notify her when the five cadet witnesses were departing Space Station Cy-7. According to the boarding information, they were leaving on the seven o'clock p.m.

transport. Magdalena used her computer system and called in Emma Ragnarsson from the main dining area of the Rosenburg mansion.

The Ragnarsson family had always been part of the make-up of Magdalena's mercenary team. Many of the offspring of Dell Ragnarsson, who was a ruthless killer in his own right, were sent off to the best universities to learn how to work in legitimate careers. Ellis Ragnarsson was sent to law school and was now a successful trial lawyer as a partner with Alfred Rosenburg, III. Ella Ragnarsson had studied private security and criminal investigations. She was now chief of security for the Baroness Hotel chain. Eva Ragnarsson had become the owner of a space craft rental agency after earning her degrees in banking and finance. Dell Ragnarsson, Junior, had followed in his father's footsteps and trained daily to be the best assassin money could buy. Emma Ragnarsson had done the same as Dell. Emma had killed over a dozen people that Magdalena knew of. There were probably many other Ragnarsson offspring that had been kept secret from the Rosenburg's. Dell Ragnarsson was a man that valued his privacy, especially for his familial ties.

Emma looked similar to her sister Ella in height, hair color and build. Emma spent all of her spare time either in the gymnasium training or practicing martial arts or learning how to put together explosives and weaponry. She was also an avid reader and had grown to be as brilliant as her sister Ella.

Emma walked into Magdalena Rosenburg's private office and shut the door behind her.

"Have a seat." Magdalena told her.

"You found them?" Emma asked as she sat on the burgundy colored couch.

"Yes. They will be leaving from the space station on the seven o'clock Transport," Magdalena informed her. "Those five cadets are not to set foot on the planet of New Edinburgh. Understood?"

Emma nodded, "And the other passengers on the Transport?"

"They are not my concern," Magdalena said coldly. "Do what must be done."

Emma stood up quickly and let herself out of the office, she had worked with Magdalena long enough to know when the woman was dismissing her.

Les Gillis was trying on several suits in the fitting room of one of the large clothing stores on the space station mall. Yuri Gorski and Jen Staszko were walking around the men's clothing section, looking for outfits to give Gillis to try on, when Lieutenant Garrison walked toward them.

"Now what?" Staszko hissed under her breath when she recognized the security chief.

Garrison stopped in front of the two cadets. "May I have a word with you?"

"It is a free Empire." Gorski said sarcastically.

Garrison pulled out of his breast pocket a small diskette in a hard protective plastic holder. He handed the disk to Gorski.

"What is this?" Gorski asked.

"Everything." Garrison said. "I downloaded the entire Love-Easter file on that disk for you. I thought you should have the file, to do with as you will."

"Why are you doing this?" Gorski wanted to know. He was suspicious of the motives of the space station security chief.

"Why?" Garrison repeated. "Because what happened to your friend was wrong. And because a lot more will be coming your way."

"What does that mean?" Staszko asked.

"It means that some powerful people want this whole case to be swept under the rug, nice and neat." Garrison said. "I like you kids. I am really sorry about your friend. I do not want the same fate, or worse, to happen to you. Use the information wisely. Don't trust anyone. Do not tell anyone else that you have this information. Watch your backs at all times. You understand me?" Garrison was looking around as if he expected to be followed.

"It is a cover up then?" Gorski deduced.

Garrison only nodded. "I must go. I wish you kids the best. By the way. I listed all five of you as passengers on the seven o'clock transport. Do not board that ship. I listed you as bait. Be mindful of the news reports. If you hear of any disaster or accident regarding the seven o'clock Transport, then you will know for certain that you are in danger. Leave by some alternative method as soon as you can. It is not safe here."

Before Gorski or Staszko could ask another question, Garrison left them. He moved quickly through the store so that they could not follow them. Yuri Gorski put the disk in his pocket.

CHAPTER SIX

Drew Harrison finished his last class for the day. He made his way out of the lecture hall and walked toward the male dormitory building. He was going to meet Dominic Andolini so they could follow Gorski's instructions and begin to investigate the Baroness Hotel chain. Harrison walked out onto the main courtyard of Clovis Academy. In the distance, the orange United Nations flag flew proudly. Harrison took a moment to admire the campus, the large dormitory buildings, twenty lecture buildings, one lecture hall was one hundred thirty floors high. The large landing strip was off in the far distance. There were several firing ranges, weight rooms, martial arts training facilities, pilot simulation rooms and computer labs.

Harrison saw many cadets and professors walking from building to building, rushing to make their next class. Some, like Harrison, had finished their last class for the day. Harrison remembered his first day at the Clovis campus. His mother and father pushed him to attend, wanting their son to follow father's footsteps as an officer in the space command. He arrived, resistant to the idea of being a military service man. But on his first day, just below the large flag pole, he met Julia Steiner. For Harrison, it had been love at first sight. He and Steiner became inseparable in no time. Their relationship lasted for almost three years. Steiner had even joined the Gorski Gang with Harrison during their first year at the Academy. There were six members then. Yuri, Drew, Julia, Marco, Dominic and Drayton. Les Gillis came along during that first year as did Mary Lincoln. Some had called them Mayhem Eight. Soon Michel Evart joined the group as did Yesenia Guevara. Frank Glenn, Dia Cho and Felicia Essex were upper class cadets that had become honorary gang members. Gorski and Harrison became roommates that first year and remained together all the following years. Gorski had grown to be Harrison's best friend.

Harrison still could remember the night he and Stiener caught Gorski and Lincoln in bed together. Then Dray became an item with Guevara. The following year, Guevara and Steiner brought in Sophia DuBravac, who was immediately drawn to Gillis. All was wonderful during those early years. The next class came along, and then the next. The group changed. Members left and others joined. The break up between Guevara and Love-Easter had been horrible for everyone. They were both beloved members of the Gang.

Harrison found he was walking slowly as he reminisced. He knew that this was no time to lollygag around. He picked up the pace and made his way across the courtyard. He always looked for Steiner, hoping to catch a glimpse of her. He never stopped loving her. Harrison was well aware the Steiner was dating one of the Collins boys. Harrison respected Steiner's decisions and did not interfere. But every fiber of his body told

Harrison to fight for the girl. He knew that fighting Collins would not bring Steiner back to him. He had to let time do its' work and heal his broken heart.

Harrison smiled when he saw Dominic Andolini approaching him. As always, the Italian gave Harrison a bear hug.

"Change of plans." Dominic told Harrison. "My brother is at the medical emergency room. There was some sort of accident during their training today."

Harrison felt immediate concern for his friends. "Marco, is he..."

"Marco is fine!" Dominic assured him. "It was some of the other cadets. I heard there was a casualty."

"Who?" Harrison was concerned. He knew that the Rhinehard brothers, Fenster, Mejia and Lincoln were on that training.

"I do not know." Dominic told Harrison. "That is why we must hurry over to the emergency facility so that we can find out."

Dominic did not wait for Harrison to agree, he was walking quickly toward the hospital building. In the distance, they could see several hundred Allen Corporation fighter type model CC76A2's approaching the landing strip for final descent. Dominic and Harrison began running.

They arrived at the entrance to the Cordell Hull United Nations Hospital Emergency waiting room to find Marco

Andolini and Jurgen Doernitz sitting next to each other. Both had worried looks on their faces. Doernitz and Marco had spent the last hour and a half getting to know each other as they waited for the doctors treating Tina Martinson. Marco knew that other cadets had hazed Doernitz. After today, Marco would make sure nobody assaulted young Doernitz again. His impressions of the younger cadet were that he was a great pilot and an honorable man.

The lobby of the hospital waiting room was practically empty. There was another couple several seats away. There were several rows of empty seats. The walls smelled like bleach. The blue floor and the white walls were tiled with an occasional picture of the Glorious Leader surrounded by signs to direct people to certain areas of the hospital. Dominic came and hugged his brother. Marco quickly hugged Harrison.

"What happened?" Harrison asked.

"One of the cadet pilots decided to become a cowboy and take on a pack of Verburgt." Marco told them. "Amir al-Nasser was killed."

"Amir? Dead?" Dominic was stunned by the news. Al-Nasser had never been a part of Gorski's Gang, but he was well liked by everyone. Dominic had especially liked al-Nasser in that they shared a passion for collecting rare weapons. They occasionally would trade items among themselves and attend trade shows together. "How?"

Marco sighed, "Amir was trying to protect Tina Martinson. She had crashed in the Forbidden Region. The Verburgt attacked Amir's ship. He was eaten alive."

"He just got married, again. I met all of his wives. His two kids. His children are adorable." Harrison sat down rubbing his temples with his fingers. "He was such a great father to them. They were always together."

"By the way, this is Jurgen Doernitz." Marco said. "Jurgen that's my brother Dominic and Drew Harrison."

"Pleased to meet both of you." Doernitz said.

Dominic shook his hand. "And what part did you play in all this?"

Doernitz began to open his mouth to speak but Marco answered for him. "This kid is one hell of a pilot. He used his tow cable to create a barrier to protect Tina from the Verburgt. It was a fantastic bit of piloting."

"But you did all the dangerous stuff." Doernitz said. "Marco, I mean cadet Captain Andolini, landed on the surface, left his ship, fought off about a dozen Tree Spiders and a giant earth worm, outran a pack of Dozal and saved the girl." It was obvious that Doernitz admired Marco for the bravery he had shown under pressure.

Marco laughed and put his arm around Doernitz shoulders. "Call me Marco. We fought side by side. The formalities are out the window now, kid."

"Uh, guys." Harrison said as he watched a medical Doctor approach them.

"Who brought in the girl, Tina Martinson?" The Doctor asked. Her name tag read Harding. She was wearing a light blue uniform, with her feet covered by white slippers and her hands were covered by plastic, blood stained gloves.

"We did," Marco said as he stood up, pointing his thumb at Doernitz.

"I am Doctor Harding." The woman said. "I am sorry to tell you that cadet Tina Martinson slipped into a coma."

"What?" Marco was beside himself in disbelief. "But she was just in shock. Jurgen and I flew her here in less than thirty minutes flat. How?"

"Please, sit down." Doctor Harding told him. "Tina Martinson suffered from blunt force trauma to her head. She had a hematoma in her brain. You saved her life by getting her to us as fast as you did. We are doing everything we can for her. Now, I fully expect her to come out of the coma. She is going to survive this, but only because you two got her to us so quickly."

Marco nodded. "You had to operate on her?"

"Yes. But she is going to be fine." Harding assured him. "We had to repair a slight skull fracture and relieve the pressure on her brain from the hematoma. The surgery was a success. Had you gotten her to us later, she might not have survived"

"Thank you for everything you did for her, Doctor." Marco said. "I hear the training ships landing. We should go."

Dominic watched as his brother stormed toward the hospital exit. Dominic and Harrison had seen the look in Marco's eyes before. Someone was going to answer for the day's events, for the injuries suffered by Martinson and for the death of Amir al-Nasser. Marco was intent on being the one to exact the punishment. Dominic ran after his brother with Harrison on his heels. Doernitz did not know what was about to happen but followed Marco out of loyalty.

Marco was running toward the air field as the cadets were landing their ships by flight. He went straight for the landing area for "A" Company. Marco could hear Admiral Seward calling out his name. He ran past Porfirio Cardenas and ignored his questions regarding Martinson. He was running from ship to ship, looking at each cadet climbing down the side of their craft.

And then, Marco saw the object of his rage. Angus McWilliams. He had already removed his helmet from his enviro-suit. Marco charged as McWilliams stepped on the ground. He could hear McWilliams bragging to another cadet pilot about his downing a Verburgt. Marco already disliked McWilliams. They had tangled several times in the past. McWilliams had been one of the Bragg faction at the Academy. In the past, it was just bar fights. Now it was personal.

"McWilliams!" Marco yelled to get his attention.

McWilliams turned around to see Marco charging him. McWilliams realized by the look in Andolini's eyes that this was not a social call. Marco threw a right cross and hit McWilliams in the nose. The force of the blow was enough to break the cartilage in McWilliams' nose. Blood spattered down the face of the cadet.

McWilliams staggered backward, his left hand instinctively covering his nose. He was seeing stars and felt as if his head had exploded. McWilliams held up his right hand as Marco threw another jab with his right hand, connecting the abdomen of McWilliams. Marco was ready to let loose a flurry of punches when Harrison and Dominic pulled him away from McWilliams.

"Let go of me!" Marco yelled as he struggled with his brother and Harrison. "He got Amir killed! Tina is in a coma because of this idiot!"

A crowd of cadets had gathered, watching McWilliams get what was coming to him. Even McWilliams' best friend, James Cobb, was unwilling to step in and stop the fight.

"At ease!" Admiral Seward demanded. All of the cadets stood at parade rest. Marco calmed down when the retired Admiral moved in between him and McWilliams.

"He assaulted me!" McWilliams pointed at Marco.

Seward walked over to McWilliams and reached out with his right hand and grabbed his broken nose between his index and middle finger and twisted it. McWilliams screamed in agony and fell to his knees.

"You think that is painful?" Seward yelled at McWilliams. "Think about how painful it was for Cadet al-Nasser to be eaten alive! Think about his children growing up without their father! You abandoned your wing man to die!" Seward released McWilliams. "Cadet McWilliams, you are expelled. I will notify the Marine Corps and the Army that you are, by binding contract, to report for duty as a Private within twenty-four hours. Now get the hell out of my sight before I let Andolini here finish what he started!"

McWilliams stood up and began running when Marco made a move toward him. Seward began barking orders at the cadets. "Turn in your enviro-suits and hand lasers to the supply officers! Tomorrow we will have a debriefing about the mission at 0600 hours! Move out!"

The cadets began running to the supply buildings. The Andolini brothers, Cardenas, Doernitz, Harrison and Mary Lincoln remained with the Admiral.

"Sir, Tina Martinson is in a coma." Marco informed Seward.

Seward waived his left hand in Marco's direction. "Son, you do not have to justify your actions to me. I wanted to stand back and let you kick that sniveling little coward's ass in front of everyone. Now, all of you, go turn in your supplies. Captain Andolini, cadet Doernitz, you two really showed something out there today. I am damn proud of all of you."

Seward then began walking back to the tower where his offices were. He was going to go visit the married students' quarters, find Amir al-Nasser's family and break the bad news to them.

"Sorry, I lost my temper." Marco said to the others.

"You only did what the rest of us wanted to do." Lincoln told him. "It reminded me of the Marco of old." Lincoln hugged him.

In the distance, they could see Mejia, the Rhinehard brothers, Fenster, Cara Perez-Guerrero, Jack and Melissa Harcourt watching. There was concern on all of their faces.

Marco smiled at Lincoln. "April is cooking tonight. Why don't you join us?" He turned to Cardenas and Doernitz. "You two, why don't you come as well. You both really did well out there. I was impressed by what you did."

Cardenas shook Marco's hand. "My wife probably already has dinner ready for us. Can I take a rain check? Some other time perhaps?"

"Yeah," Marco was smiling at Cardenas. In the four years that Marco had been a student with Cardenas, they never spent much time getting to know each other. Marco liked Cardenas' composure out there in the Forbidden Region. His decisive leadership made a difference in the life of Tina Martinson. "I would like that. How about you Jurgen?"

Doernitz looked at Cardenas, "Well, I normally eat with my sister and Porfirio every night. I am sure she has cooked a lot of food for us."

"That's right," Harrison said, snapping his fingers. "You two are related by marriage."

Cardenas nodded. "Jurgen, why don't you go with them? Freya will understand. You need to socialize more with your classmates here."

"Are you sure?" Doernitz asked.

"Go have some fun Jurgen. After today, you deserve to relax." Cardenas told him.

"Okay," Doernitz said. "Tell Freya for me, where I am?"

"Great!" Marco put his arm around Doernitz. "I promise you will be safe with us kid. You really were spectacular in how you handled that fighter in such tight surroundings."

"I was really scared out there." Doernitz admitted suddenly. He did not know why he said that.

"We all were." Lincoln assured him.

"How do we get through the fear? Doernitz asked.

Cardenas put his hand on the shoulder of his brother-in-law. "Just have faith, Jurgen."

Doernitz walked with the Andolini brothers and was introduced to the others by Marco. Doernitz, while shaking everyone's hands only noticed that Melissa Harcourt was smiling at him. Cara Perez-Guerrero was eyeing Doernitz with lust in her eyes.

FORBIDDEN REGION

Cardenas felt proud of his brother-in-law. Perhaps now the other cadets would finally accept him and the hazing and bullying would end. Cardenas began walking across the airfield toward the married student dormitories. He was looking forward to seeing his wife and children. He felt lucky to be alive. He prayed to the Lord as he walked, thanking Him for the blessings of his wife and children.

Les Gillis walked out of the bathroom to see Yuri Gorski and Jen Staszko waiting for him. Gillis was wearing a black double breasted suit with a French blue dress shirt and black dress shoes. Staszko had picked out the clothes. She smiled approvingly.

"You look very sexy." Staszko told him.

"I'm jealous." Gorski added.

"You two are certain this will keep this woman's attention?" Gillis motioned with his hands at the suit. Gillis has always been much more comfortable in jeans and sweats. But, he was willing to do anything to get to the truth as to what had happened to Drayton.

"I think you are going to knock this girl dead." Staszko told him as she stood up and brushed some lint off of the black suit with her hands. "You just be yourself. You are the most intelligent student in the entire Clovis Academy. You are going to be a fantastic catch for some woman out there. So be confident. And make sure you ask her many questions about herself."

"Like what?" Gillis wanted to know.

"Like, her family." Staszko began. "Ask her about her education, her time at school. Ask her what her favorite type of music is. Her favorite color and what she likes to do in her spare time. Stay away from religion and politics on the first date. Do not push her to speak of subjects she is uncomfortable with, just move on to something else."

"So, I have to see her again after tonight?" Gillis asked. "I thought I was supposed to get all of the information I could out of her tonight."

"Poor you." Gorski laughed. "That woman is hotter than molten lava and you are upset that you might have to date her more than once? Look, Les, it will take time to get this lady to trust you. She is a professional and obviously educated. Just have fun with her tonight. Get her contact information at the end of the dinner, suggest that you two meet again and leave it at that."

"What if she volunteers information regarding what happened?" Gillis asked.

"Then you can go into it." Staszko told him. "Play everything cool. You can do this."

Gillis nodded. Gorski was right. Penelope Smith was hotter than molten lava. He was filled with mixed feelings that he drew this assignment. He was still in love with his last girlfriend, Sophia DuBravac. He missed her company and wondered why she had ended their relationship. But since she had broken off her ties to him, Gillis had been in the market for a quality lady to help heal his loneliness. During the two years that he had spent with DuBravac, Gillis grew to love her more than anything in the world. He needed a new woman to fill the void in his life left by her sudden departure. He found that he was actually looking forward to getting to know this manager of the Baroness Hotel. He looked at himself in the mirror when he heard Staszko admonish him to brush his teeth.

CHAPTER SEVEN

Ellis Ragnarsson was a handsome man with good muscle tone and a chiseled chin. He had dozens of lovers that he would choose from to pleasure himself. He had women, men, Kotek's and an Akarzdamedian slave woman at his home. His favorite sex toy was one of the female lawyers that worked in his law firm named Jada Ying. She was smart and a great trial lawyer. She worked hard and won cases for his firm. But she was also spectacular in his bedroom. Ellis Ragnarsson did not like the fact that his sister Ella had interrupted a session of love making with Jada Ying to request his services. He received the distress notice over his Holo-com device. The message from his sister was simple, he was needed to clean up a problem on Space Station Cy-7. He gave his apologies to the delicious and desirable Jada Ying so that he could shower and get dressed in his best business suit to take care of family business. He kissed Ying good bye as he left for his private space craft.

Alexi Khartov was not a physically fit man. He was sixty years old, financially well off, and had a wife substantially younger than he was. His business was thriving. Khartov found a niche in buying and selling fur coats and leather jackets across the Eight Solar Systems. He had made enough profit to purchase his own Fenster Corporation Transport Ship Series XII. He paid cash for the craft, brand new. He was able to accumulate substantial inventory of the fur coats and jackets. But, Khartov had let his body go. He ate foods full of fat and cholesterol. He was a chain smoker of cigars, drank ale, beer and whiskey on a regular basis. He had a huge stomach and was two hundred pounds overweight.

So, when the military intelligence police arrested him on Space Station Cy-7 and accused Khartov of murdering a young man, that was physically fit and had completed training as an elite Spetsnaz soldier, he was speechless. He was not a killer. He had decided to travel to New Edinburgh to negotiate with a manufacturer to purchase jackets and hand bags constructed out of the skins of the indigenous dinosaurs of that planet. He believed, and his wife Alejandra agreed, that exporting such product to the other planets and colonies could be very profitable. Being arrested on such a business trip was the absolute last thing he would have ever believed would happen.

Khartov protested the charges. He swore that he was innocent, that he was not even on the space station at the time of the killing. So, the security guards and investigators began drugging Khartov. He was later shown the signed confession that the investigators swore he had signed in their presence and view. He demanded legal counsel and the reason his wife had not been brought to visit him. Khartov demanded to see a judge and better treatment. And in response to all of Khartov's demands, the criminal investigators placed him in something they called "The Tank."

Khartov had never heard of such a thing before. But he learned quickly that the Tank was not a place for the faint of heart. In under twenty-four hours, he had been beaten and raped by male inmates repeatedly. Most of the designer clothing Khartov had been wearing when thrown into the Tank had been stolen from him. He now sat in the corner of the large cement cell, in his underwear with bruises all over his body. He had never been treated in such horrific conditions in his entire life. He reached a point where he wanted to die and end his suffering.

As Alexi Khartov sat on the floor of the cold cell, contemplating how he would commit suicide, he heard his name called out. He struggled to his feet and he slowly walked to the metal bars at the front of his cell. He saw two armed guards and a man in a business suit. The man reached through the bars and handed him a small three inch by five inch white business card. He read it. "Law Offices of Rosenburg and Ragnarsson. Ellis Ragnarsson, Attorney at Law." He looked at the man in the suit. He had short blonde hair, blue eyes, stood over six feet tall, had a chiseled body, high cheek bones and sported a mustache. His suit was expensive. Khartov knew clothing and this man before him knew quality.

"Who are you?" Khartov asked.

"Ellis Ragnarsson, Mister Khartov. I am your lawyer." The sharp dressed man reached through the bars and shook

Khartov's hand. "Can we go to one of the conference rooms and discuss your case?"

Khartov nodded. "Yes, please. Get me out of here."

The guards opened the bar doors and walked in and grabbed Khartov's arms and dragged him out of the cell. He was taken down a long corridor, through a door to his right and then several paces down the new hallway to a small ten foot by twenty foot room. The room only had a six foot long metal table and three metal chairs. The four legs of the table were bolted to the floor. Khartov was physically placed in one of the chairs by the guards. The guards handcuffed his right wrist to one of the table legs. Ellis Ragnarsson sat down across the table from him. The guards left and closed the door behind them.

"Good." Ragnarsson the lawyer said. "Now we have privacy. I have looked over your case file. You confessed to murder."

"No!" Khartov banged his left fist on the table. "They drugged me. I did not kill anyone. Why won't anyone believe me?" He had tears rolling down his cheeks. The man was frustrated beyond his patience level. "Please. You have to tell them I could not have done this thing. I was not even here on the station when the crime occurred. They say I killed someone that had a black belt in some fancy martial art! Look at me! I cannot even lift twenty pounds! Please help me!"

Ragnarsson listened to Khartov's ranting without emotion. He sat, staring at the accused criminal, blinking only twice. "Are you finished, Mr. Khartov?"

"Yes. Can you help me?"

Ragnarsson drew a deep breath. "So, you feel you were framed?

"Yes."

"And you will insist on a trial?"

"Yes." Khartov slammed his left hand on the table.

"You understand that the victim in this case was born into a prominent family? There will be considerable news coverage of your trial." Ragnarsson stood up and began pacing around the tiny room.

"I do not care!" Khartov told the lawyer. "I demand a trial. I am not guilty!"

"I could arrange a plea bargain arrangement in which you accept a light sentence of twenty-five years." Ragnarsson told Khartov. "If you agree, the prosecution will withdraw the indictment seeking death by hanging."

"What?" Khartov was stunned. "They want to hang me? I did nothing wrong!"

"But you can avoid death by pleading guilty and doing a twenty-five year sentence on Cootron." Ragnarsson told Khartov. "I have tried many cases, and I highly recommend you take the deal, do the time and you will be out before you know it."

FORBIDDEN REGION

"I am not guilty!" Khartov yelled. "I plea to nothing!"

Ragnarsson nodded. "Of course. I am only doing my job. I have an ethical obligation to explain to you all of your options. So, you wish to risk death? All or nothing?"

"I will never say I killed that young man!" Khartov was assertive in his statement.

"Too bad." Ragnarsson told Khartov sarcastically. "You are such a delightful fellow. Now, this is where things get tricky. You see, you should never pull a weapon on your lawyer in a jail. That shows poor decision making skills."

"What the hell are you talking about?" Khartov demanded. "I have no weapon to pull!"

Ellis Ragnarsson was smiling at Khartov and pulled out a hand laser from his pants pocket. "This weapon. You stole it off of the guards when they dragged you in here. You tried to kill me. I had to fight back." Ragnarsson fired two kill shots at the wall across from Khartov which caused black and brown scorches on the concrete.

"You are crazy!" Khartov yelled, ducking his head down.

"You missed me twice. Then I struggled with you and the laser went off." Ragnarsson said as he shoved the barrel of the hand laser into Khartov's chest.

Ragnarsson pulled the trigger as Khartov began screaming. The entry wound in Khartov's upper chest was only about an inch radius. But the exit wound in Khartov's back left a foot long chunk of flesh vaporized. Khartov's heart was gone; pieces of his spine and rib cage were also annihilated by the deadly laser. Khartov's head slumped to the side. Ragnarsson pushed the chairs over and began yelling for the guards. The two jail employees rushed in and saw the confessed murderer, Alexi Khartov, dead. Ragnarsson handed the laser over to one of the guards.

One of the two guards was covering his mouth and nose due to the smell of burnt flesh and meat. A laser on kill setting would blast holes in targets such as brick walls or trees. But for humans, it would burn through the flesh, bone and muscle. The stench was difficult for some individuals to handle. Especially if it was the first time one was exposed to the foul odor.

"I think he stole this off of one of you." Ellis Ragnarsson told them. He should have taken the deal, the lawyer thought to himself. "He fired two shots at me and jumped me. It just went off in the struggle. I am really sorry."

The two guards checked Khartov's pulse. "He's dead," one guard stated the obvious.

"I have some other clients that I need to visit today." Ragnarsson said, straightening his tie. "Can you summon some more guards to escort me while you two dispose of this mess?"

It was the perfect assassination. All lawyer-client interviews were confidential. No surveillance of any kind was allowed. Ellis Ragnarsson was certain that the Rosenburg's would be satisfied with his efficiency in dealing with Khartov.

He waited as two other uniformed guards arrived and escorted him back to the Tank.

"I need to speak to three new clients that my law firm was hired to represent." He told the guards. "They were arrested for assault, battery, conduct unbecoming an officer and attempted sexual assault."

"Names?" One of the guards asked.

"Boris Ilyasova, Jericho Griffin and Heinrich Jahn."

The two guards led the lawyer back to the cell blocks.

After several rows of cells were passed by, the guards stopped at a large cell. The guard called out the three names Ragnarsson had requested. The three men walked toward the bars.

"Who are you?" Boris Ilyasova, the former Lieutenant Commander of the science vessel *Colorado* demanded. His face was disheveled and his clothes were torn from fighting. There were seven other prisoners in the same cell. One was naked on the floor, lying in a pool of his own feces and urine. Another man was lying in the left corner, his face bloodied from an apparent fight with one or more of the other inmates. He seemed to not be breathing. The other five were sitting against the wall, saying nothing.

"I am Ellis Ragnarsson, your lawyer. I was retained to represent all three of you in court. And, I was also asked to offer each of you employment." Ragnarsson said, handing Ilyasova his business card.

"What kind of work?" Ilyasova wanted to know.

"Flying ships." Ragnarsson said with a smile. "Doing exactly as you were trained to do. I work with a corporation that has need of pilots. The pay for each of you will be three times the amount you were making in the space command. You get benefits. And, my employer can arrange for you to have all the women you want and need."

The three demoted officers looked at each other and nodded.

"How can we accept your offer if we are locked up in here?" Griffin motioned to the bars and the cell around them.

"Simple." Ragnarsson said. "All three of you will plead guilty to Conduct Unbecoming an Officer. I will get the Judge to drop all of the other charges against you. The court will place you on something called Deferred Adjudication. It means you e-mail a probation officer once per month and don't break any more laws for a few years. Once the years pass, the charge of conduct unbecoming is dismissed. The good news is that if you agree to what I just said, all three of you walk out of here, free men, today."

"We are in." Ilyasova told the lawyer. He was still reeling from his bad luck. Most women did not struggle to get away from him as Mejia had. She was the first to actually complain about him. Due to that little whiney witch, he lost his comfortable gig as chief pilot on a science cruiser. The offer made by the lawyer before him was a gift from the stars. Ilyasova could not thank the lawyer enough.

"Great." Ragnarsson smiled and shook their hands. "I will file the papers with the Judge and you should be out in two hours. I will be waiting for you at the release point. Transportation to your new employment has already been arranged."

"How do we thank you?" Jahn asked.

"By accepting the employment offer you have already thanked me." Ragnarsson told them. "You will be paid very well, but you will have to work hard to earn the money."

Ellis Ragnarsson asked the guards to escort him to the jail magistrate to arrange for the release of the three pilots. What Ragnarsson did not tell Ilyasova, Griffin and Jahn was that they would all three be transporting slaves, illegal weapons, smuggling criminals and illegal drug and taking young men and women to have their body parts harvested to keep others immortal. Based on the past record of the three pilots, he knew that they would have no difficulty following that type of life. They seemed to have no values whatsoever. They might make good pilots for the Rosenburg's, but Ilyasova, Griffin and Jahn would never qualify as geniuses.

CHAPTER EIGHT

Emma Ragnarsson moved with the crowd of civilians, pilots and soldiers as she entered the Docking Bay of Space Station Cy-7. She had a large back pack slung over her right shoulder. She was wearing a black pair of utility pants, black boots and a dark burgundy sweater. Her hair was tucked under a black baseball style cap. After a few minutes of walking around the area and inspecting the numerous space ships, she located the seven p.m. Transport. Some of the passengers were already boarding her. Emma slowly made her way to the ship. She was careful to not move too fast or slow, as that might attract attention. Using the bill of her baseball cap, she kept her face hidden from the security cameras in the ceiling of the docking bay.

Emma had been well trained in the art of assassination. The trick was to either frame someone else or make it look like an unfortunate accident. She had determined that this was best to be made to look like an accident. Space craft malfunctioned and people died as a result.

FORBIDDEN REGION

She walked around the side of the space craft and inspected the perimeter. She was certain that no one was watching her. She quickly slid underneath the belly of the Transport. She pulled open her back pack and pulled out the magnetic explosives and the timer. She attached the explosives to the ship and then the timer. She set the timer for one hour. That would ensure that the explosion would destroy the Transport when it was clear of the space station and well before it was in the atmosphere of New Edinburgh.

Emma Ragnarsson slid out from the bottom of the craft after checking to see if any feet were around where she wanted to exit. No one detected her. She calmly walked out of the Docking Bay. She went to visit her sister Ella to share a drink and a laugh or two.

Massimo's was packed. The Italian food restaurant had sixty tables with a seating capacity of two hundred thirty customers. The waiters wore tuxedos as did the bar waitresses. Gillis arrived early for his date with Penelope Smith (Rosenburg). He was taken to his table and ordered a glass of water. And he waited. Seven o'clock came and went. He waited till fifteen after the hour and decided he should just leave. He had been stood up, the woman was not coming.

Gillis looked over to the two top table in the corner where Yuri Gorski and Jen Staszko were sitting. He shrugged and motioned toward the empty seat at his table. Staszko motioned with her head for Gillis to look at the door. He did as she directed. And there she stood. Penelope was wearing the blue dress she promised. Her slender back was exposed. The straps of the dress were spaghetti thin and her shapely and firm arms and shoulders looked perfect. The dress cut low around her chest. Gillis caught himself admiring the woman's ample cleavage. The dress was tight around her waist and legs. She had put her hair up and was wearing diamond earrings that Gillis guessed were a minimum of two carats. She looked magnificent. Many men turned their heads to get a better look at her as she seductively walked toward Gillis.

Gillis stood and greeted her with a polite hug, pulled out her chair and helped her sit down. As she settled in, Gillis sat back in his chair. He glanced over at Gorski and Staszko who were both trying to be discreet.

"You are enchanting." Gillis told her.

Penelope smiled at the compliment. "Thank you. You look very handsome. Is that suit new?"

"Yes," Gillis admitted. "I bought it especially for tonight. I left my other dress clothes behind at the Academy."

She sensed that was her opening to interrogate Gillis, subtly, so that he would give her some useful information. "So what led you to want to attend the Academy and agree to serve all those years as a soldier?"

Gillis unfolded his napkin and put it in his lap. "I wanted to see other planets and outer space. I felt at age seventeen that traveling to another planet to attend the Academy was the best way for me to accomplish that. I was accepted at several colleges and selected Clovis Academy. I liked the campus, the history, the faculty and the fact that it was the newest planet that humanity had occupied successfully with an Academy."

The waiter arrived and Penelope asked Gillis if she could order for both of them. Gillis nodded. She looked up at the waiter and smiled. "We will take a bottle of your house Moscato, an order of Lobster Ravioli as an appetizer. For our entree we will share a Lasagne al Forno and a Vegetarian Primavera."

"Soup or salad with those meals ma'am?" The waiter asked.

"Your house salad please." She answered. The waiter bowed and left. She turned her attention back to Gillis. "So, why be a soldier? I am certain you could have attended one of the private universities. They are all over the Eight Solar Systems."

"True." Gillis admitted. "I could have done that. But, as a child I always wanted to be a man in uniform. It was a dream I had. Being in my senior year I had to make another decision, whether to serve my term in the space command or go on and earn my doctorate."

"And what did you decide?" Rosenburg asked as the wine arrived. The waiter opened the bottle of imported Italian 2411 Moscato. He poured for the two customers and placed the bottle in a thin metal container that would keep the contents of the wine bottle cool.

"I decided to go on to achieve my doctorate." Gillis answered. "I already have been accepted at the Advanced College of Military Intelligence on Sikorsky's Planet." Gillis sipped his wine glass as his date did the same. The wine was delicious. "And you, Penelope? Why did you decide to work in the Hotel business?"

She had been prepared for the line of questions. She knew he would probe her to learn all he could about the Baroness Hotel. She smiled and drank some more wine. "Well, it was never my ultimate plan. I wanted to go into the finance world. Inter-stellar banking was my first love. I like money. I enjoy turning money into investments and seeing those gambles turn a profit. I am, as they used to say on old Earth, a true capitalist."

Gillis smiled at that and they both laughed. And so the conversation continued as the salads arrived. Penelope kept her answers vague, trying not to give the Irishman too much information to go on. Soon the Lobster ravioli was delivered. As they ate and talked, Penelope found herself liking Gillis more and more. He was genuine, open, funny and brilliant. The men Penelope had dated over the years were very shallow and lacking intelligence. Gillis possessed all the qualities that other men did not have. Most importantly, he was not a killer for hire as were some of the men that had wooed her in the past. As the main entree arrived, Penelope was certain she wanted to see this man again. She would have to convince her father not to order any attempts on the life of Gillis. That would be difficult to do.

She learned that Gillis and Love-Easter had lived in the same dormitory room for the last three plus years. She questioned him about how much dedication it had taken for the two men to care for their black and white domestic cat named Cosmos. Gillis could play the six and twelve string musical instrument known as a guitar. He also held a black belt in a martial art. He came from a large family and was the first of his siblings to actually take a space craft ride and leave Earth's orbit. His favorite meal was something called Shepherd Pie and he preferred nice wines as opposed to ales, beers or liquor. He was proud of his heritage and spent a few moments during the conversation to convince her that the Irish saved Western civilization during the Dark Ages. She also discovered that Gillis was fiercely loyal to his friends.

Gillis learned only vague facts about Penelope. He learned she was extremely intelligent and business oriented. She would not speak of her family, saying only that she had little to do with her parents. Gillis found that she had a great sense of humor and she was beautiful. Gillis knew it was going to take many "dates" to get to know this woman.

The food was gone as was the wine. Penelope had ordered an Italian coffee as her final drink. Gillis ordered a plain coffee and politely rejected the offer of cream or sugar.

"So, Penelope, how do I find you?"

"Here on the space station," she responded simply.

"No, I mean, how do I contact you?" Gillis began, trying to find the words to let her know that he wanted to see her again without coming off as too aggressive. "I find your conversation stimulating. I would like to communicate with you via three dimensional computer feed. I was wondering what your access identification code was so I could contact you."

She smiled at him and concluded that satellite mails would be harmless. Her security codes were ironclad and the best hackers would not be able to find out her true identity from her work mail. "Penelope@Baroness.Cy7."

"That is simple to remember," Gillis observed. "May I contact you in the morning, before I leave to attend my first lecture?"

Penelope nodded, "Call on me anytime. I normally work form six a.m. till six p.m. But I am off on Mondays."

"Then I will keep in contact with you," Gillis said as he saw Evart and Papanikolaou were waiting to get his attention. Gorski and Staszko were also motioning to Gillis that it was time to leave.

He sighed as he hated to leave the beautiful woman behind. But he knew that Evart and Papanikolaou had been trying to arrange their flight out and clearly it was time to return to Clovis Academy.

Gillis stood up and asked the waiter for the bill, which was three hundred thirty Empire Dollars. Gillis gave the waiter four hundred Empire dollars and told him to keep the change. He walked over to Penelope and put his hands on her beautiful shoulders.

"Fare thee well, Penelope my dear. I must be going away," Gillis told her and he gently kissed her on the cheek. She stood and gave Gillis a passionate kiss on his lips. The kiss lasted only a few wonderful seconds before she pulled away.

"Thank you for a wonderful evening," She told Gillis and walked out of the restaurant. Gillis was stunned that she had kissed him. He walked toward his friends with a broad smile on his face and saw that they were with Arch Frazier.

"Damn, Les! How did you get a woman like that? She could be Miss Universe!" Frazier told him and was promptly hit on the shoulder by a jealous Papanikolaou. Frazier cleared his throat, "Well, she would be runner up to Elektra."

They all watched Penelope Smith (Rosenburg) step on the elevator. She looked over to Gillis and smiled at him. The elevator doors slid shut.

"I think she likes you, Les," Staszko observed.

"I guess so," Gillis said softly.

"Let's get out of here," Gorski ordered. The six cadets followed him toward the Docking Bay.

The seven p.m. Transport left the space dock of space station Cy-7 about fifteen minutes late. There were two pilots and forty-seven listed passengers of men, women and a few children. There were two Kotek passengers as well that boarded the doomed flight. About forty minutes after the Transport flew out into space, the charges attached to the belly of the craft detonated. The chain reaction of the explosion caused the space craft to rip to pieces. Those that did not die in the explosion perished as they were swept out into the space vacuum.

There were no survivors.

The news of the disaster was initially reported as an engine malfunction.

The fifth floor of the woman's dormitory at Clovis Academy was bustling with activity. April Mejia, Lila Zapata and the Rhinehard brothers were playing "host" to a crowd of cadets. The menu was enchiladas, refried beans, Spanish rice, chili con queso, tortilla chips and salad. Mejia and Zapata were prepping and cooking as Klaus and Rolf were serving plates to their friends. Dominic Andolini had his arms around Harumi Shigeta, as they shared a margarita. Marco Andolini was standing next to Jurgen Doernitz and Mary Lincoln, relating the day's events in the Forbidden Region to a crowd of underclassmen. Doernitz and Lincoln did their best to impress on everyone Marco's heroism when he rescued Martinson.

Drew Harrison, Jack Harcourt, Mia Nguyen and Sophia DuBravac were sitting on one of the beds in Mejia and Shigeta's dorm room, eating the delicious food. All four had margaritas on the floor to wash down the home cooked meal. In the bathroom were Dirk Fenster and Ann Harcourt, operating the margarita machine, handing out full glasses of the concoction to all that entered the dormitory room. Melissa Harcourt and Cara Perez Guerrero were among the women listening to the story of the daring rescue.

The Academy separated the women from the men in separate dormitory buildings, but there were no restrictions on spending the night. Several couples would come, get a plate of food, a drink and leave. Doernitz went to put his empty plate in the recycle bin in the hallway. He thanked Mejia for her hospitality and her great food. Doernitz was told to come back the next night as another one of the other cadets would be cooking something for dinner. For the first time since he enrolled as cadet at Clovis Academy, Doernitz felt like he belonged. All of the cadets were treating him nicely and with respect. He felt happy that he was finally accepted. He was ready to leave when he felt a set of arms wrap around his right arm. He looked to see who it was and saw Melissa Harcourt holding him.

"Don't leave yet, fly boy," Melissa told him.

"Why, what is going on?" Doernitz asked her.

"What is going on is that I want us to get to know each other better." She whispered while guiding him down the hallway, holding his right arm close to her. "See that door on the left?"

Doernitz nodded, "Yes."

"That's my room. We can talk in there."

She opened her door and led him inside. Doernitz looked around the room as she walked past him and he heard the door shut. He was about to make a comment about the room being nice when Melissa wrapped her arms around his neck and kissed him. Doernitz was surprised by the aggressive move since he had only been kissed once before in his life. That was when he was seventeen. Melissa proved to be a far better kisser than the first girl.

She slowly pulled her head back but kept her arms around Doernitz. "Have you ever been with one of us?"

Doernitz could feel her pressing her body against his. He had instinctively wrapped his arms around her waist. "You mean have I ever been kissed by a woman?"

Melissa smiled, "No, silly. Have you ever made love to a Child of Athena?"

Doernitz thought for a second about his answer. His sister Freya told him to always tell a lady the truth, no matter what. So he did. "Well, I have never actually, you know, I've never been with anyone."

Melissa kissed him on the cheek, "So, I will be your first then?"

Doernitz watched as Melissa Harcourt pulled off the half-shirt she was wearing, exposing her breasts. She took his hand and led him toward the bed. Doernitz willingly followed her. He was very attracted to Melissa so she had no problem seducing him. Doernitz savored every kiss, every caress. He felt his heart racing as she placed his hands on her body, encouraging him to kiss her all over. When Melissa began unzipping his flight suit, he was all hers. They made love over and over again.

At some point in the late evening the students heard a blood curdling scream down the hallway. The conversations ceased and the crowd ran out into the hall. They all saw Flora Evart, Michel Evart's little sister come out of her room, crying and yelling over and over again: "They killed my brother!" Flora's roommate, Supreet Patel, was trying to calm her down.

Harrison, the tallest person on the floor, got to Flora first. "What happened, Flora? What are you talking about?"

Harrison had his hands on Flora's shoulders, holding her still as he waited for her response. She looked up at him, her eyes filled with tears. "The news reports. They said the Transport from the space station blew up. They listed the names of the dead! Michel was on that ship! Drew, They all died!"

Mary Lincoln gasped. Everyone else was silent until Klaus darted into Mejia's room and instructed her computer to broadcast the latest news. The three dimensional image of an attractive female news reporter appeared and was relaying information of the tragedy of the Transport explosion. Mejia was standing next to Klaus, who instinctively put his arm around her shoulders as she was cried.

The reporter listed the names of the dead. The names came in alphabetically by last name. Everyone heard Michel Evart's name, then the names of Les Gillis, Yuri Gorski, Elektra Papanikolaou and Jen Staszko.

The silence on the fifth floor was deafening, interrupted only by the sounds of the many weeping cadets. Marco Andolini slid to the floor, covering his eyes to hide the tears. Shigeta and Dominic were hugging each other in an attempt to give one another comfort.

No one could believe the news. First Love-Easter and now this.

After the initial shock of the tragedy began to sink in, the crowd dispersed as the news had ended the festive mood. Soon, Mejia was alone in her room, cleaning up. Her door was still open which enabled her to hear the footsteps behind her. She turned to see Klaus in her doorway.

"Thought you could use a little help," Klaus told her.

"I am tired of cleaning." Mejia told him. "Life is too short to waste, Klaus Rhinehard."

"I agree."

Mejia gave him a devilish look. He was very handsome. She admired his thick blonde hair, blue eyes, and his muscular, toned body. Mejia enjoyed the way he looked at her. She felt at that moment, that their being together was destiny. "Then what are you waiting for? Close the door and bed me."

Klaus swallowed hard as those were the words he had wanted to hear from her for the longest time. Mejia noticed that the man hesitating and concluded that perhaps he needed a bit of convincing. She began unbuttoning her blouse, smiling at him. Not wanting to miss a second of her undressing for him, walked backwards and closed her door. He watched her pull her blouse off her shoulders and drop to the floor. She moved toward him and they began kissing.

He ran his hands over her body, kissing her neck and shoulders. "Which bed is yours?'

"Who cares?" Mejia said as she was pulling off her bra. "Pick one and throw me on it."

Klaus did as she commanded. He had wanted her for the longest time ever since he first laid eyes on her. For him, it had been love at first sight. He had her on the bed, each pulling the others clothing off.

As he was making love to her, he let the words spill out during the passion. "I love you."

"I love you too," Mejia answered him. She had never felt so much for a man before. It was the first time that the two had fallen in love with another.

After their passion had been spent, Klaus was lying on top of Mejia, gazing into her beautiful brown eyes. He was kissing her gently and she him as he would run his hands through her hair. He suddenly realized that there would be a possibility of a pregnancy since he had not taken any precautions. The Security Council had outlawed contraception, birth control and abortion due to the pressing need of more humans to populate the conquered and terra-formed planets. Klaus knew how much Mejia longed to become a Space Command officer and a fighter pilot. If she was to become pregnant, she would be grounded until she gave birth.

"April, if you become...." Klaus began.

Mejia cut him off, as if she read his mind. "Don't worry. I never thought I would be in love, ever. I would be so honored to give birth to your child. So, take me whenever you want. I am all yours. And if we have a child, or even many children, my love for you will only grow that much stronger." She ran her fingers through his hair as she spoke to him. She remembered that her mother warned her that one day, she would find the one man that would make her feel this way. Mejia had never been happier.

Sophia DuBravac had been told of the deaths on her walk back to her dormitory room. She maintained her composure until she made it to the end of the stair case leading to her floor. She began weeping, unable to contain the flood of pain she felt due to the death of the man she loved. She wiped the tears from her face as she walked down her hallway to her room. She shed more tears, as if her eyes were a waterfall. Several of the other female cadets saw DuBravac and stood against the wall, not wanting to get in her way. DuBravac's reputation for defending herself was vast. No one wanted to be in her sights.

DuBravac stopped at her door to her room and found that she could not speak the words to her security computer to open the sliding doors. She leaned against the hallway wall and let out a blood curdling yell of remorse. She had lost Les Gillis forever. He was gone.

DuBravac wanted to hide and get away from all of the staring eyes of her classmates.

Daniella Day was present, covering her mouth with her hand with a look of concern on her face for DuBravac. Day wanted to go to DuBravac to comfort her, but held back due to the well-known propensity for violence that DuBravac had displayed in the past. When she had first arrived to the Academy, Day had interacted with DuBravac. Day had dated one of the Gorski Gang members named Dirk Fenster. The relationship between Day and Fenster had been short lived. Day would never forget the evening she witnessed DuBravac, Julia Steiner, Yesenia Guevara, Mary Lincoln and Jen Staszko wreak havoc on several grown men during a bar fight. The women had been out numbered about three to one. The women prevailed. Day recalled hiding under a table in that seedy bar as the others engaged in the brawl, the likes of which she had never seen before or since. DuBravac was a woman that could handle herself. Day decided to stand back not wanting to suffer DuBravac's wrath, if there was any to be handed out.

There were dozens of women just watching her. DuBravac wanted to lash out at them. But she knew her pain was not their fault.

Lila Zapata was the only one with the courage to approached DuBravac. She reached out with her hands and wiped the tears from her cheeks.

Zapata did not care about DuBravac's alleged propensity to fight. All that mattered was that her friend was in emotional pain. Zapata hugged DuBravac close to her.

"I am so sorry," Zapata told her softly.

DuBravac wept on Zapata's shoulder.

FORBIDDEN REGION

CHAPTER NINE

The *Blues City* was a fast space craft due to modern technological advances and a few additional booster rockets installed by her owner. Giles Lancer was able to make the flight from Cy-7 to New Edinburgh in less than three hours. He had done so on many occasions. Most of the trips had been to assist cadets or civilians that needed a lift. During the flight Lancer informed the cadets that all of them, save Frazier, were dead.

Gorski leaned forward when Lancer made that statement. "What do you mean we are dead?"

Lancer slapped Gorski on the leg. "Relax kid. You will get home safe. That's what you all paid me for. You kids were on the news. The last Transport from Cy-7 blew up and your names were on the list of victims."

"What?" Staszko was surprised by Lancer's announcement.

"How many casualties?" Evart asked.

"I think they reported forty-nine dead," Lancer informed them. "You guys want to use the communication broadcast to contact your families and friends? Let them know that the news is wrong? I am sure they are all very worried about you."

Frazier nodded, "Yes, we should contact the others. If they think you are all dead..."

"No," Gorski said firmly. "No. We wait until we land to contact everyone."

"Why?" Papanikolaou was shaking as she was concerned about her family on Greece. Gillis watched as Frazier put his arm around her.

"Because I think that whoever killed Dray will want us dead," Gorski said. "And Lieutenant Garrison agreed with me."

"Why would you buy into such a conspiracy theory?" Evart asked.

"Because we saw six attackers. The authorities said only one killer was involved. The lone attacker confesses. The security observation feed in the hotel was cut during the time of the attack? And now, just by coincidence, the transport ship that had our names registered as passengers blows up? Add it up guys. Too many unexplained events in such a short time period. I am very suspicious."

Lancer heard what Gorski said. "You referring to the cadet that was killed? Easter?"

"Yes, Drayton Love-Easter." Gorski answered.

"Well, check this out," Lancer stood up. "The guy that confessed attacked his lawyer in the Tank. His own lawyer killed him in self-defense."

"Which means no trial," Gillis added. "No more publicity."

"So, we cannot let our friends know we are alive because why?" Papanikolaou wanted to know. "They must all be worried sick. My family in Greece will want to hear from me. I need to call them."

"I agree Elektra," Gorski said calmly. "We will contact everyone once we are safely on the ground. Let the people behind all this think they got us. Up here in space, they will track our communications. They could blow this ship away with a rocket and they would, if we let them know we are alive."

"So we are dead," Evart said without emotion.

"That's too bad," Gillis shook his head. "I was just beginning to like all of you."

Lancer laughed and looked at Frazier, "I should have charged you double. You kids are dangerous. Don't worry about a thing. I am a master at covert actions. You all will get home safe tonight. Evart, you are a pilot, right?"

"Yes," Evart answered.

"Good, take the controls and keep the ship on the current trajectory and flight plan," Lancer told him.

Evart smiled at the opportunity to fly the nicely kept vessel. He stood up and walked to the pilot's seat. "Captain Evart at the controls, ladies and gentlemen."

Lancer looked at Frazier and Papanikolaou and motioned for the two of them to descend the metal stairs to the lower level of the ship. The couple followed him down stairs.

Gillis leaned forward to face Gorski and Staszko, "Yuri, your father is in charge of the military occupation of New Edinburgh. He is going to be furious if you do not call him, Michel's uncle will be as well. We have to get word out somehow."

"I am thinking about how to do just that, Les." Gorski leaned his head back to rest it on the chair he was sitting in. "When we land I will call my father. Michel will contact his uncle and he will make sure we get back safely. We need to let Drew and the others know we are okay as well, but we do it after we land. We will be surrounded by friends and military service men and women that are under my father's command. All of our friends are cadets that have training in self-defense and weapons. We are safer on the ground."

"I agree," Staszko said but failed to add that for the first time in her life, she was genuinely afraid. She had faced tense moments during her childhood as a gypsy in Eastern Europe. Her family had been shot at, spit on, had rocks thrown at them and asked to leave several locations. But each time, Staszko felt that the situation could be handled safely since the terrain, the perpetrators and the solution were all known. The current predicament she found herself in was one of uncertainty. The people that were trying to kill them had not yet been identified, and that was the scariest component to her.

Frazier and Papanikolaou returned with Lancer each carrying three foot wide and tall plastic containers in their hands.

"Set them down here," Lancer told them. They put the three boxes at the feet of Gillis, Gorski and Staszko.

"What is this?" Gillis asked.

"Weapons," Lancer told them. "I know Fenster is good for the money. You kids need to be able to protect yourselves. These boxes have knives, hand lasers, flame darts, thermite grenades, stun darts, hand and leg binders, a few garrotes, heat sensors, motion detectors and some poisons."

"Really?" Staszko was wide eyed as she inspected the contents of the boxes.

"Damn right." Frazier smiled. "If there are people after us, then we need to be able to fight back. The Academy only checks out weapons to us from the supply depot. What do we do at night when someone attacks?"

Gorski opened one of the plastic containers and saw a large stock of weapons. "If we get caught with these on the campus, we will be expelled and prosecuted."

"Better to be judged by twelve than carried by six," Papanikolaou commented bluntly.

FORBIDDEN REGION

It was against the laws of the Glorious Leader, Vladimir Sikorsky, for any civilians to own, possess or carry any form of firearm. Only soldiers and those authorized by the Glorious Leader were allowed to arm themselves. Gorski and Gillis wondered silently how Lancer had access or even clearance to have the weapons in his possession.

"Look, as far as we know they only targeted five of us," Gorski said. "Arch you are not involved in this. I don't want you carrying any of these weapons."

"The hell I am not involved!" Frazier countered. "Dray was my friend too."

"I did not mean it that way, Arch." Gorski said. "These people, whoever they are, have not targeted you. Just the five of us and I want it to stay that way. Arch, think about your education and your future. If the Professors catch you on campus with any of this, they will kick you out of the Academy and send you to the enlisted ranks."

"I know the risks," Frazier said. "But we have to do something."

"You already did do a lot. You got the five of us safely off of the space station. We will do a lot more things, too. But putting ourselves in jeopardy of expulsion is not one of them." Gorski turned to Gillis, "Les, the regulations specifically prohibit certain items. Are any of these not on the Security Council or Academy ban lists?"

Gillis smiled and understood where Gorski was going. "Yes. The binding cords are not banned. Knives are allowed as long as they are not for offensive usage."

"That's how I am able to have my knives on campus," Staszko told them.

"Right," Gillis said pulling out the items from the plastic container. "Binding cords, knives are fair game. Lasers are out, they are banned. So are the flame darts and thermite grenades. The heat sensors and motion detectors are not banned." Gillis held up an item as long as a ball point pen, "These stun darts are not banned. We could carry these in our pockets, completely concealed. If we are attacked, you stick this in the persons' muscles like their neck or leg or shoulder. Press the button on then end and they will be paralyzed for hours."

"I have never heard of that weapon before," Papanikolaou said, picking up a stun dart and inspecting it.

Gillis nodded, "That is because the Rosenburg Corporation that manufactures them has not sold them to the Space Command yet. They are strictly being sold on the black market."

Lancer was nodding, "How do you know so much about these things?"

"I read a lot," Gillis responded and concluded silently that Lancer was much more than a simple owner of a transport ship. He had to have some contacts in the illegal weapons trade.

"So, these stun darts. Are they lasers?" Frazier asked with one of the small weapons in his hand.

"No," Gillis shook his head. "Several years ago some explorations officers stumbled onto some poisonous snake like creatures in the jungles of Planet Cootron. The venom of these creatures attacks the human nervous system, causing a form of paralysis. You can feel and sense everything happening to you and around you, but you cannot move. So, the Rosenburg Corporation scientists created a way to harness the venom in these pen shaped weapons."

"If we take the knives, arm and leg binders, heat sensors, motion detectors and stun darts, how much will it cost us?" Gorski asked.

Lancer crossed his arms and looked each of the cadets in the eye as he spoke. "You kids have to promise to never tell a soul what I showed you today. The knives are free. I have thousands of them, so take all you want. The stun darts run $500.00 Empire Dollars each. The binders are $15.00 each. Heat sensors are $1,000.00 apiece as are the motion detectors. Pick out what you need. You can pay me later."

Gorski stood up, "I don't know how to thank you for this."

"Thank me by staying alive," Lancer told them. "You kids are good customers and I need the business."

CHAPTER TEN

Colonel Nikolai Gorski had been working all day and night. His office was his home away from home and was a cramped forty feet by thirty feet. To the officer, the office seemed to be a prison. The promotion that he felt he had so richly deserved had passed him by and the four walls seemed to keep him trapped like a tomb. He had a black desk, plush roll back chair and chairs in front of his desk for visitors. His walls had his degrees and awards framed for all to see, a Bachelors Degree, a Master's Degree and a Doctorate in War Tactics. He had been awarded the Medal of Valor twice for his actions during the Dinosaur War. His Certificate from completing Spetsnaz training was his proudest achievement since that was earned while he was still with his beautiful wife, Melita. Her picture was displayed prominently on his desk. Although she had died over fifteen years ago, he still loved her and missed her greatly. His friends and co-workers had attempted to introduce him to single women over the years, but he found that no other woman could compare to his lost love.

FORBIDDEN REGION

Since Melita's death, Gorski had been raising their two children alone. Yuri, the oldest who was in his last year at the Clovis Academy, and Piotr, who would be starting his first semester at the Academy next year. His two sons were very different. Yuri was the smarter of the two, outgoing and had many friends. Piotr was more of the quiet type and never really socialized that much. Piotr never got into trouble, but Yuri gave his father migraine headaches with his antics.

Colonel Gorski had been mobilizing his Marine troops to perform mock invasions of the Southern Continent. Gorski knew that soon he would be ordered to begin the Second Dinosaur War in the Southern Continent. He had recommended to General Welker of the Space Command that the southern advance be delayed until the military could completely secure the Northern Continent. Even though Gorski had met the demands of the Space Command and established eleven major colonies on the Northern Continent, there was still over eighty percent of the land mass occupied by the dinosaur population. Gorski and his top officers agreed that securing the entire north continent should be the priority.

The Space Command Generals on Sikorsky's Planet disagreed with that assessment.

Gorski asked the computer to turn on the news broadcast. A three dimensional holographic newswoman appeared before him. She was from the military news service. She was reporting the death of the killer of Cadet Love-Easter.

The killer, Khartov, had attempted to kill his lawyer with a stolen laser pistol. The lawyer, Ellis Ragnarsson, had been fortunate enough to disarm Khartov. Khartov had been killed in the struggle.

The other news was that the Transport Shuttle from Space Station Cy-7 to New Edinburgh had exploded just before entering the atmosphere of the planet. All aboard had perished. Gorski was signing orders that his Supply Captain had left on his desk when he heard the list of the casualties. One of the lost was his son, Yuri Gorski. Colonel dropped his laser point pen on the desk top in stunned disbelief.

"Computer, replay list of casualties," Gorski requested.

The list was re-read. It had been no mistake; Yuri had been listed as a passenger on the space craft. Gorski closed his eyes and put his head in his hands. He had such high hopes for Yuri. The Colonel felt as if someone had kicked him in the gut. In all of his battles and training, nothing could prepare a parent to lose their child.

Major Sigebert Evart darted into Gorski's office, breathing heavily. Evart's office was on the floor below Gorski's and he had run up the flights of stairs as soon as he received the call from his nephew. "Colonel, the news!"

Gorski looked up at the Major, "Yes, I heard. My son and your nephew were on that transport ship. How do I tell Piotr that his older brother his dead?"

Evart shook his head, "Sir, we do not have to tell anyone anything. I just got a call from the Private Flight Pad north of the city. They were not on the Transport!"

"What?" Gorski stood up.

"Sir, they took a private ship. Michel just contacted me. He asked that only you and I know and that we come to escort them back to the campus right away."

"What the hell for!" Gorski rumbled. "My son couldn't contact me and let me know? I am sitting here going through emotions I had never felt before!"

"Sir, they think that they are being targeted." Evart responded in defense of the cadets.

Gorski put on his camouflage fatigue jacket, "Targeted by whom?"

"By the people that killed their friend Drayton and blew up that Transport," Evart answered.

"Okay, let's get a transport and meet them at the airfield," Gorski told the Major as he checked the charge level on his laser pistol. "I wonder what kind of poggie shit my son and your nephew stepped in this time."

The back offices of the Baroness Hotel were normally quiet in the evenings. There would be a few security guards monitoring the cameras, a cleaning person, and the food service personnel for room service issues. But this night was different since there was cause for celebration. Ella Ragnarsson, chief of security for the Baroness Hotel, had invited some guests to bring closure to a successful operation. They were assembled in the Executive Conference Room which was about eight hundred square feet. The Executives of the Hotel normally would meet in the mornings around the rectangular table and discuss the business. But this night, they would not be discussing Baroness Hotel business.

They would be toasting to the elimination of their enemies.

Ella had several bottles of champagne on ice sitting on the center of the large table. There were a dozen crystal champagne glasses, hummus, pita bread, dolmas, bread with sausage, prime rib slices and a block of Swiss cheese with crackers and a cheese slicer. Ella's brother, Ellis was present as was their sister Emma. Alfred Rosenburg the Third, Ellis' law partner, was carving some cheese to go with his drink. The four of them were sipping on the expensive champagne, waiting for the guest of honor.

Penelope Rosenburg entered the back security area of the hotel after her palm scans cleared. She was still thinking about her date with Gillis, recalling how charming he had been in a naive way. She had changed out of the dress and was now wearing a pair of black slacks and a tight light purple sweater. She had been summoned by her father to meet him in her Executive Conference Room. She had no clue why or what the meeting was about. Her father normally would not leave the Ranch unless the proverbial poggie dung had hit the fan.

FORBIDDEN REGION

As Penelope entered the Executive Meeting Room she was greeted by cheers and applause of congratulations. The three Ragnarsson siblings applauded for Penelope. Her older half-brother, Alfred, handed her a glass of ice cold champagne.

"What is this about?" Penelope was laughing, feeling relieved that her father was not there to scold her for some reason or another. She sipped the drink in her hand. "Did we make additional sales records?"

"No," Alfred told her. "We completely wiped out any further issues due to Caine's screw up. We are home free."

"And that is why father is coming here?" Penelope was suspicious. Her father was a cruel and unstable man. She still remembered how he brutally murdered Cush, one of his own sons, just to keep the rest of the sibling group in line.

Alfred downed another gulp. "No, my dear sister, father is not coming. We just told you that so you would come and join us. I know how you value your sleep time."

Penelope relaxed a little and turned to Ellis, "So what brought you here? More clients?"

Everyone began laughing at her question. Penelope gave everyone a confused look since she did not understand what was so funny.

"She does not know!" Ellis said gazing at Penelope's chest. He put his arm around Penelope and smiled at her, "My lovely lady, the eye witness, Khartov? He tried to attack me and I had no choice but to defend myself." His voice was sarcastic.

"Poor man died in the fight. All self-defense of course." Ellis was holding Penelope really close to him. Before Penelope had all of her cosmetic surgery, Ellis never gave her time of day. Now that she resembled a beauty queen, the lust in his eyes was obvious to one and all. Every moment he was around Penelope, he would try and pour on the charm. Penelope would never forget the fact that the handsome lawyer never even told her 'good morning' until after all of her surgical procedures and physical therapy sessions were completed.

"You killed Khartov?" Penelope asked. "Why? Was that really necessary?"

"I did the fat pig a favor," Ellis announced, taking a drink from his glass. "He was going to spend at least forty years on the prison planet, doing hard labor. Death was an early Christmas gift from me to him."

"That is why we are celebrating?" Penelope asked.

Emma nodded, "That and the other loose ends we tied up today."

Ella cut in, "Lieutenant Garrison will no longer be a problem for us. While he was with the search and rescue in space, his enviro-suit uniform malfunctioned. Poor man, he died slowly. That is what he deserves for screwing me on my desk and then screwing me by betraying me." Her voice sounded cold as ice. Penelope knew that Ella probably killed Garrison for some personal satisfaction. The Ragnarsson's normally killed for money. But they also would kill for their own vendettas. And may the Gods help you if the Ragnarsson's wanted your life for a personal reason. Your death would be painful.

Penelope took another drink of her champagne. She felt sorry for Garrison as he seemed to be a decent and honorable man. Of course he allowed himself to be seduced by Ella. Few men could resist her. But, Garrison was also from law enforcement and he could not let the Love-Easter case go. His dedication to his job and to his oath cost him his life.

"Wait a minute!" Penelope was cognizant that Ellis was still holding her close to him and began thinking of an excuse to get away from him. "Why were search and rescue and Garrison out in space?"

Emma began jumping up and down like a young school girl wanting to get her teacher's attention. "Because the Transport with all the eye witnesses blew up! They were all on the seven p.m. flight. One bomb and they were all gone."

Penelope took in a breath as she heard the announcement. She knew Emma was wrong since Gillis and his friends were still on the space station at seven p.m. "All of the eye witnesses? Are you certain?"

Emma was jubilant and clapped her hands. "Yes! I got them all with one bomb."

"Are we good or what?" Ella asked her, much too proud of herself.

"So then, what is next?" Penelope asked.

"Nothing," Alfred answered. "Ellis and I are going back to the Ranch with three new pilots we recruited. You and Ella stay here and keep the Hotel making money. Emma will report back to her father for more freelance work. All is well that ends well, so they say."

Penelope moved out of Ellis's embrace. She did not want to tell what she knew of Gillis and his friends. Penelope really liked the young cadet from Ireland. If she told this group of their failure, they would move immediately to correct the error and finish the job. Penelope judged Gillis and his Russian friend, Gorski, as being very smart lads. She hoped that they were both smarter than her family and the Ragnarsson assassins. Penelope became worried as she realized she was secretly rooting for the other side against her own family. If her lack of complete loyalty was ever discovered, she would be tortured and killed as was her older brother Cush and she had no desire to end up like Cush.

"To success!" Ella raised her crystal glass high.

They all drank in unison. The celebration continued for a few hours until Alfred and Ellis told all that they were leaving.

Ellis wrapped Penelope in his arms and kissed her on her lips, "I will be coming back for you soon."

Penelope felt his hands slide down her back and onto her buttocks. Ellis moved to kiss her again and she turned her head to the side so that he kissed her cheek instead of her lips.

"What is your problem?" Ellis said in a whisper. "I could be the best thing that ever took you to bed."

"Or you could be the worst," Penelope pulled out of his embrace.

"I will be back for you, Penelope and when I return you better be ready to get down to business. Our parents are negotiating terms for us to become a couple. You are already mine and don't know it yet." Ellis informed her as he left. Penelope secretly hoped that she never had to see Ellis again. She shuddered at the thought of her father using her in such a manner, to marry her off for a business arrangement, especially to a rogue villain like Ellis.

Penelope stayed up for a few hours more and drank with Ella and Emma. They made small talk about the past, specifically growing up on the Rosenburg Ranch. The issue of Caine's screw up and the investigation over the cadet murder was finished for them. Penelope knew full well it was not over. She had always been a good judge of character. Her family was full of psychotics, social deviants, narcissists and sadists. The Ragnarsson assassins were only loyal to money. Gorski and Gillis were loyal to their friends and to each other which meant that the cadets would stand together, even when the odds were against them.

CHAPTER ELEVEN

The chief of criminal investigation division for the Space Station Cy-7, Charles Bennington, was notified by his computer that there was another emergency. Bennington had been sleeping. He woke up and stretched his arms over his head.

"Computer, brew me up some coffee," Bennington said. "What is the nature of the emergency this time?"

"The search and rescue team has been working on collecting the bodies and wreckage. Lieutenant Garrison went with them to investigate. He was suspecting arson or sabotage. He and his security guards were collecting pieces of the ship when there was a uniform malfunction."

"Who had a malfunction?" Bennington asked as he buttoned his shirt.

"Lieutenant Garrison is dead," the Computer reported without emotion. "Your presence is requested at the forensic examiner's office."

Bennington sat down on his bed, thinking of his friend. "Damn."

Colonel Nikolai Gorski and Major Sigebert Evart arrived at the private airstrip on the northern end of Clovis City in a dark blue transport ship, a Fenster Corporation Nova Transport Model 778, which was capable of carrying up to fifty persons. Gorski and Evart brought along a squad of eleven loyal Marines, each were in combat fatigues, carrying laser rifles and their utility belts had laser pistols, thermite grenades, flame darts and large knives. After Major Evart landed the ship, the eleven marines jumped onto the metal and concrete strip and secured the perimeter.

About a hundred yards north was the ship *Blues City*. Colonel Gorski and Major Evart moved quickly and they crossed the hundred yard distance in no time. Giles Lancer met the officers at the entrance to the ship with a laser rifle, ready to fire.

"Not one step further!" Lancer warned. "Slowly, walk under the lights." He motioned to the solar powered light post ten yards from his vessel.

Lancer waited for the two men to comply. He looked at their faces. "Colonel, I served under your command in the Dinosaur Wars. I don't know if you remember me. I remember you. It was an honor to fight under your leadership. On my ship are six scared kids, one of them is your son. We called the Major so you could come get them."

Colonel Gorski cleared his throat, "I am in debt to you for watching over my kid. Can we come in and see them?"

Lancer lowered his laser rifle, "Please. Hurry, before dawn comes."

Gorski walked up the ramp and shook Lancer's hand. Major Evart did the same. The two Marine officers quickly walked up the spiral stair case to the second level of *Blue's City* and they found in the seats the six cadets. Yuri Gorski stood and hugged his father. Michel Evart did the same with his uncle. A look of relief seemed to wash over the faces of the other four cadets. Yuri had profound respect and love for his father and Michel felt the same for his uncle. Both of the cadets felt release from the anxiety and worry over their situation when the Colonel and Major arrived. "Thank the Stars you are safe!" Colonel Gorski said with relief. "We need to get all of you to a secure location."

Major Evart was holding his nephew close, "What did you all get involved in this time?"

"One of our friends was murdered," Michel Evart said sadly. "All of us here, save Arch, were witnesses. People are dying up in that station and it is all connected."

"Or, it is all a terrible coincidence." Colonel Gorski said. He and Major Evart had discussed the allegations made by Lancer and Michel Evart on the flight to the airfield. Both of the

Marine Corp officers knew that sometimes there are coincidental events that the "conspiracy theorist" news media would blow out of proportion. Colonel Gorski had personally lived through it twice, the first was when the news media scandalized the death of his wife, Melita, claiming that one of the Doctors on her mission had damning evidence against the Secretary General and thus he was marked for execution. The second event was during the Dinosaur Wars when one of, then Captain Gorski's, platoons got separated from the rest of the Brigade in a battle. The platoon only had three survivors. The conspiracy writers believed that there were members of the platoon that had information regarding the famous Nour family, so their deaths had to be arranged. Colonel Gorski did not believe the conspiracy theory writers.

Major Evart and Colonel Gorski had come up with some preliminary strategies, just in case this specific situation was not a conspiracy theory. They had decided that they would afford the five cadets protection in a manner that would allow them to continue their studies at the Academy.

"Frazier, I want you to go back to your dormitory room. Tell nobody about this. Let everyone believe these five are dead for now." The Colonel walked up and down the hall of the ship as he spoke. Staszko realized that she had seen Yuri do the same when he was thinking.

"What are we going to do?" Papanikolaou asked as she moved next to Frazier.

Colonel Gorski faced the six cadets, "Frazier is going to go back to school. I am told you hired this ship to go get the other five. That was very brave of you son. I would love to have a man like you in my Marine Corps Brigades."

"I am majoring in Explorations and Geology," Frazier said.

"Nobody is perfect, Cadet Frazier. But when you see the light and decide to become a Marine, you let me know." Colonel Gorski muttered. "You other five will be my guests for the night. In the morning, we will meet with Admiral Seward and Dean Harvard to determine how you can resume your studies."

"How will we be safe if there is someone out there trying to kill all of us?" Staszko asked. "How do we fight back against an unknown enemy?"

"We will have to wait for them to make a mistake, if, and only if, there really is a threat." Colonel Gorski said. "Most likely, all of this is just coincidence."

"Kid, tell your father," Lancer said from behind them.

"Tell me what?" Colonel Gorski asked.

"Well, the only one on the station that seemed to believe us that there was more than one killer was the security chief of the space station, Lieutenant Garrison. Before we left, he gave me this!" He pulled out of his breast pocket the disk with all of the investigation files. "Garrison believed us."

"And now Garrison is dead," Lancer announced. "Enviro-suit malfunctioned while he was helping gather evidence of the transport explosion."

Colonel Gorski grunted and motioned for the cadets to follow him. "Let's go. Mr. Lancer, thank you for everything."

"My pleasure, Colonel." Lancer shook his hand.

"Where are we going?" Michel Evart inquired.

"You five are going to a safe location," Major Evart told them. "You are staying in my quarters and the Colonel's.

The group followed the Colonel. He turned to the cadets as they walked, "After we meet with the Dean and Seward, I will be assigning each of you armed protection. Under no circumstances do any of you go anywhere without the person I will assign to you. Also, you are to tell nobody that your protection is from me. They will be posing as Academy cadets and they will become your new best friends. Understood?"

"Yes sir," Yuri Gorski stated for everyone.

"Good. I will have some of my best criminal investigation division detectives delve into the Love-Easter case." Colonel Gorski stopped at the steps of his personal transport. "I know each of you have friends, close friends. Do not tell them a thing. You might place their lives in danger if, indeed, this is a real cover-up as you are alluding to. I mean it. Yuri, not a word to your Italian friends or Drew. Michel, even your sister Flora must be kept in the dark. Elektra, not a word to your roommate in the dormitory. Jen, Les, the same applies to the two of you. Say nothing, not one word of your suspicions. You kids got lucky this time."

"We understand sir," Michel Evart promised.

"Good. You better understand. If something big is going on here, and I believe that each of you think that the transport explosion and Dray's death are connected somehow, so in case you are right, the Academy will be under full time surveillance." Colonel Gorski motioned with his arm for the cadets to board the Marine transport. Major Evart waived his hand for the eleven Marines that had secured the perimeter to board. The eleven ran quickly to the space ship for their trip back to the United Nations Building.

Yuri Gorski took Jen Staszko's hand in his and he took in a deep breath of the clean air. For the first time in days, he felt safe. The lovers followed the Marines as the sun began to rise in the horizon. They had outsmarted their enemies and a new day was beginning. Gorski pulled Staszko into his arms and kissed her passionately. Frazier and Papanikolaou embraced each other as well; kissing each other like there was no tomorrow.

Michel Evart laughed, kneeled down onto the pavement and kissed the ground. He stood up and looked at Gillis, "I would kiss you Les, but you are not my type."

Gillis looked at him as if her were offended, "So, if I were gay, you would not find me attractive?"

Evart kept laughing, "No. Sorry, my friend."

Papanikolaou was laughing and hit Evart on the shoulder. "Now just a second there, Michel! I saw Sven! He looked like he hadn't bathed in weeks and probably had fleas! You would kiss a guy like Sven and not a clean cut handsome man like Les?"

He shrugged, "I told you that a year ago Sven looked better."

"Holy Hera, Michel! A dead Poggie would look better than Sven!" Papanikolaou pointed out.

Gorski and Staszko were laughing now. They both realized that it was the first real care free jovial moment that they had in the past three days. Gorski hoped that they would share many more moments such as this in the future.

"I guess we are safe," Staszko whispered to him.

"For now," he responded as he held her close. "For now."